MURDER
AFTER
TEA-TIME

MURDER
AFTER
TEA-TIME

by Leela Cutter

ST. MARTIN'S PRESS
New York

Library of Congress Cataloging in Publication Data

Cutter, Leela.
    Murder after tea-time.

    I. Title.
PS3553.U86M8   813' .54   81-8745
ISBN 0-312-55276-9   AACR2

Design by Dennis J. Grastorf

10 9 8 7 6 5 4 3 2 1

FIRST EDITION

*To Sherry, Diane, and especially Mark—
with thanks for all your help*

MURDER
AFTER
TEA-TIME

CHAPTER 1

IT WAS A FINE Sunday afternoon in the almost-too-charming little village of St Martin's Mere. Drab sparrows foraged among the fallen chestnut leaves that glowed in the sun like beaten copper. The conversation of passing equestrians drifted through the sparkling glass of Lettie Winterbottom's parlour window. A horse whinnied outside, as a terrier barked.

The remorseless ticking of the cuckoo above the mantel dominated the silence of the room—as clocks will—heavy with significance, like some morbid detail in the disintegration of a psychotic heroine's sanity, when nothing seems quite right afterward.

Julia inhaled the familiar smells of her aunt's house: lemon-scented furniture polish, mothballs, the piney scent of disinfectant. Aunt Lettie sighed and shakily touched a Dresden teacup to her tiny rosebud lips. Her niece Julia bit into a chocolate biscuit and sympathetically considered the vague old face. Old ladies, it seemed, sighed frequently; whereas Julia, at twenty-seven, rarely felt the inclination, even at these worst of times.

A hundred pairs of ceramic eyes stared blankly down from the mantel and china-cabinet shelves. Julia remembered believing as a child that all these frozen little people came to life at night to act out thrilling dramas while all the big people were asleep . . . typical of the fluff in children's heads.

Lettie moodily licked her fingertip and scrubbed at a spot on the tatted doily on the arm of her rocker. "I feel positively ancient, I mean, thoroughly over the . . ."

Julia munched her biscuit and waited for the end of the sentence that she knew would never come. The old girl left fragments dangling untidily everywhere these days. She had even left unfinished the concluding sentence of her recently published *Hot Cross Buns Murders*; and the publishers hadn't caught it before it went to press. So maddening for the mystery-reading public! A thousand bitter complaints had already deluged the publisher's office. It was an awkward situation, especially since Lettie could no longer make up her mind whom her detective should incriminate when he remarks to Armitage over a noble old brandy, "So, dear fellow, only one of our suspects could have had access to not only the bun tin, and the egg cozy, but the tea trolley as well, at precisely three fifteen when the postman rang . . ."

"Rubbish, Auntie!" Julia was saying. "Don't let this awful uproar get you down!" Her eyes strayed again to the knickknacks. She was trying to make up her mind which piece epitomized kitsch most thoroughly—the coy, rosy-cheeked urchin statuary or the decorative urns depicting shepherds and shepherdesses in outlandish postures of courtship.

"But you know it wasn't nearly as well-received as my previous book. I was knocked all . . ." Her high voice drifted off uncertainly, as she stared gloomily out into her garden. A blackbird, something shining in its bill, perched on the head of the gaily-painted plaster elf that squatted among the yellow mums.

"You know full well that the public is a fickle beast," said Julia.

"Yes, yes, but did you read Malcolm What's-His-Name's column? Oh! Downright cruelty! Said I was losing my . . ."

"That tiresome bag of wind! I invariably loathe every book he lauds. Honestly, no one gives a sausage for his column these days."

The corners of Lettie's grateful smile soon drooped again. "If only I could . . ."

The cumulative effect of a prolonged conversation with the old girl was of repeatedly dozing off before she could finish a sentence. Julia yawned, struggling against the torpor that was stealing over her. They sipped more tea and listened to the wind rustling around the dead grape leaves on the arbor, and the music-box-tinkling of sheep bells down the meadow.

"I'll show them I'm not dead yet!" Lettie suddenly pro-

2

claimed, smacking her teacup onto the coffee table with a clatter.

"That's the spirit!" Julia leaned over and fondly patted her birdlike arm. She really was an old pet, in spite of her maddening habits.

"I shall accept the challenge in today's post—an invitation from that remarkable Mrs Penn-uh . . ."

Julia waited a moment or two before remarking that she was unable to guess who the hell Lettie was referring to.

Lettie winced slightly, as she always did when someone used bad language in her presence. "Oh, you know—she edits that bi-monthly—uh . . . *Deadwood* . . . no, *Driftwood,* that's it. She wants me to write a serial."

"What fun!"

"Only just now I haven't an idea in my . . ."

"A locked-room mystery—those are always popular."

"But so technical! I don't know . . ." Lettie frowned and smoothed her navy wool skirt that draped gracefully around her reedlike ankles.

"A conspiracy of murderers is always jolly."

"Oh, I fancied something more romantic—a gothic, perhaps—they're as safe as houses."

"Oh, please!" Julia groaned. "Smith's has got a million of those tiresome things! Racks and racks with practically identical covers: a synthetically beautiful young woman in flowing tresses and vestments, fleeing from a brooding castle. The monotony! The gawd-awful predictability!"

"But, my dear," Lettie interjected, "Gwenna Hardcastle's *The Heart of Heathhaven* . . . or is it *The Heat of Hearthaven*? Well, anyway, it netted her forty thousand pounds last year."

"Forty thousand for that bum fodder! Incredible!"

"And inspirational. What a tidy sum for a few months . . ." Lettie's china-blue eyes suddenly twinkled at the thought of all that lovely lolly nesting comfortably in her account.

"I suppose there's something to those damned covers," Julia mused. "Symbolic of modern woman's desire for escape from the dull little brick box in the suburbs—or the drab office in the city. Lose something?" she inquired, for Lettie had begun wandering aimlessly around the room.

"Just my knitting. I find it so helpful when I need inspiration. It's the clicking of the . . ."

Suddenly noticing the time, Julia jumped up. "I'd better be off this minute, or I'll miss my train!"

Lettie opened the door for her. In the street a black terrier was in the process of bringing down a small boy from off his bicycle.

"Timothy!" Lettie shrieked. "You naughty dog!" The terrier paused. The boy, swearing handsomely, pedalled out of reach. "That same boy has pedalled past here for years. Why Tim doesn't recognize him, I can't think."

The dog ruefully watched his quarry escape, then about-faced and made for Julia's stockings with such dispatch that she barely evaded him in time.

"Tim's always so thrilled to see you, dear." Lettie chuckled fondly.

"Isn't he just?" Julia glared into the little devil's face, as she leaned down to examine her stockings. He stared up at her with eyes that glittered like buttons. His breath revealed that he had recently dined on some buried tidbit as he suddenly sprang for her face, licking her on the lips before she could dodge him.

"That's it, Tim, kiss Julia good-by."

Suppressing a shudder, Julia quickly wiped her mouth on a handkerchief. "I don't know if I'll make it next Sunday, Auntie."

"Don't you remember? Tim and I are leaving on holiday next week—to Brighton to stay with the cousins for a month."

"Right! Have a smashing time, luv. Just what you need—some sea air and not to worry about *Hot Cross Buns.*"

"Of course, dear." They hugged affectionately and Julia strode out the white picket gate.

"Young women are so frightfully athletic-looking these days," she muttered to Tim as they watched Julia's slim figure recede briskly down the lane.

A fortnight passed greyly for Julia as her little white Austin wound through London streets—from her flat to the office of *Horizons Unlimited* and back home again. The dreary rows of semi-detached houses she passed twice daily reminded her of the dreck it was her job to glamorize at her office typewriter. Semi-detached—her recent state of mind. She wasn't one of those people who thrived on routine—the comfort and satisfaction of it was lost on her. At her weakest moments, she expected to die of boredom, sprawled face down over her typewriter on some Monday afternoon, with four hours to go before the work day ended. (migod — what did she do?)

At lunch Julia dreamed over lurid travel brochures to distract herself from the greasy taste of lukewarm Wimpy Burgers. On weekends she stayed in bed late, wondering if it would be worth just packing it in and squandering her meagre savings for the lure of witty conversation with interesting foreign misfits in some far-flung, grubby cafe.

It was a Wednesday evening. Julia had only just climbed the stairs to her second-floor flat, turned on her favorite classical guitar record, and was wearily munching an apple when the phone jingled. It was one of the elderly Brighton cousins calling to say that she was "just a teeny bit worried about Lettie."

When Julia inquired if Lettie was feeling under the weather, the cousin replied, "I have no idea. What I mean to say is, I haven't the faintest idea where the dear woman has gotten to."

"But isn't she with you?"

"No, or I should know her whereabouts, shouldn't I?"

Taking a deep breath, Julia settled into a floor cushion and suggested that they begin at the beginning. The cousin obligingly explained that Lettie had arrived, as planned, a fortnight ago. But she had stayed only one week when—out of the blue —she had vaguely referred to "urgent business with her publishers" and had taken the very next train north, which was the 5:15 p.m. The two ancient sisters, concerned and slightly offended, had waited a few days before they rang up Lettie's cottage in St Martin's. They learned from the housekeeper that Lettie had apparently arrived from Brighton in the evening after the housekeeper had gone home for the day, left a cryptic note, and driven off for points unknown in her vintage Humber estate wagon.

The cousins were certain that while in Brighton, Lettie had received no calls, wires, or letters, which was why the sudden bolt had seemed so peculiar. In fact, one of them had been in Lettie's company practically every waking moment, except for the day of the dog show.

"Our rheumatism was acting up, so Lettie had to go to the dog show alone. That very evening she left."

Julia made comforting sounds. Surely a few calls would be all it would take to locate Lettie. "No doubt at her brother Richard's in Torquay."

"No, we rang Richard—as well as the Joordans, Amarantha Garsmyth, Dr Harrigan, the vicar, and the hospital at St Martin's. We were about to ring the police when we remembered you."

Julia said it was too early to call the police.

"But none of the usual people have heard from her in over a week."

"Wait a bit—the big dog people—the Crabtree-Swipes."

"They left suddenly for Canada—two weeks ago, I believe. A sudden illness in their family over there."

Julia finally managed to conclude the conversation with "Oh, listen, I'm certain she's really quite all right. I'll check around a bit and get back to you."

"You'll call the moment you hear."

"Of course."

"She's such a small woman. And what with burglars and Arabs and sex maniacs about—a body just isn't safe. Of course, plucky little Tim is devoted—but what can a terrior do against an Arab? And a woman her age driving by herself! Why didn't she take the train as usual? It's much more sensible."

Julia rang off and thoughtfully finished her apple before she dialed the housekeeper's number in St Martin's. The housekeeper couldn't furnish much information other than the exact wording of Lettie's note: "Will advise two days before returning. Cover the mums in case of frost."

"I've been beside meself with worry! But I keep telling meself at least she took that dog with her—he'd protect her against kidnappers. But what good would he be in a car smash —or a stroke? Just between you and me, I was glad to get rid of him. He's been a big problem terrifying the neighbours, he has."

Julia was only mildly surprised to learn that the housekeeper's years of fussing over Tim had been insincere. Later For a moment, while waiting for her wok to heat up, she stared abstractedly at the cleaver she'd used to dice the pork and vegetables. An uneasy feeling gripped her stomach and she succumbed to horrible imaginings. But the wok sizzled, and she scraped all the bits into the oil and shrugged. "Really! This is too silly! She's somewhere contentedly knitting away in front of the telly."

Next morning at the office Julia had just called the last name on her list and was nervously gnawing on her pencil when Gerald, her fellow copywriter, breezed in, late as usual.

"We're looking a tad green around the gills," he gasped. "Perhaps something more nourishing than erasers would help. Run out of comestibles at home? On our salary, I'm not surprised."

"It's just a little personal problem that wants clearing up."

"You mean that fascinating Teutonic boy that keeps ringing?" He mewed knowingly.

"Sorry to disappoint you, Ger, but this has nothing to do with sex. And that Teutonic boy isn't the least bit fascinating."

"That's only because you don't have anything in common."

"But you, of course, would have at least one thing in common with him. Why don't I give you his number? I'm breaking our date Friday night, maybe you can catch him on the rebound."

"Thanks for the tip, darling. But just between us chaps, if it's money, I can let you have a fiver until pay day."

"That's decent of you, but it isn't money. It's Aunt Lettie. She's vanished. I've rung absolutely everybody—not one of them has seen or heard from her in a fortnight."

"Gawd! The poor old puss has been reading too much of her own stuff."

"You're impossibly flip sometimes, Gerald," Julia muttered ill-humouredly.

"Only to hide a festering wound," he said huffily. He waved his arms in an absurdly vigourous gesture, then stalked into his cubbyhole and slammed the door. *A.e.?*

Grumbling, Julia dialed the number of the Bertrand Hotel and soon learned that Lettie hadn't stayed there in ages. Nor had she attended the Tuesday Poison Pen Society's meeting, even though it had been her turn to preside. Julia's luck finally changed when the chairman of the Germaine Arms, a respectable establishment in Hampstead, related that Miss Winterbottom had been their guest one night the previous week. She had left no forwarding address. He couldn't recall if she'd had any mail or visitors, but did supply one interesting tidbit. "We had a nice chat as she settled her account. I inquired if she was working on a new thriller. She said 'Never mind about *Hot Cross Buns*,' that only that day she'd received an inspiration for the next one, that she would entitle *Murder After Tea-Time*."

Julia dashed out of the office on her lunch hour and walked the few blocks to the office of *Driftwood*, a magazine that specialized in covers with dull seasonal motifs and articles designed to offend—and interest—no one. Julia couldn't help associating it with tedious hours whiled away in uncomfortable waiting rooms.

The name on the desk was Mr Robbins. The suit was very periwinkle, but the face was avidly heterosexual. When he heard her enter he hurriedly stuffed into his drawers the *?*

boobs-and-buns illustrated that he'd been perusing. He smiled with frank approval at Julia's attractive profile and asked hopefully what he could do for her. *why, was she sideways?*

"Julia Carlisle to see Mrs Penn-Wyant."

"I believe she has just fifteen minutes before a luncheon engagement."

"That will be sufficient."

"I take lunch then too. I hate to eat alone. Why don't we have lunch together?"

"Thanks very much, but I'm not your type," she politely replied.

His swinging singles leer halted mid-swing and dropped into a business hours deadpan.

"Proper charlie," she mumbled, passing his desk and knocking on Penn-Wyant's door.

"Toffee-nosed bitch," he murmured appreciatively through moist lips.

Penn-Wyant was a monumental woman, resplendent in several yards of grey flannel. A two-inch-long rhinestone-encrusted beetle clung to her lapel. She emanated an air of worn comfortableness, like an overstuffed couch.

". . . So I'm afraid the dear old thing forgot to tell any of us where she was off to."

Penn-Wyant nodded. "Yesterday's post brought the first installment of *Murder After Tea-Time*. It's fair stuff—more sparkle than *Hot Cross Buns*, thank heavens. At any rate, let's take a look at the postmark." She uttered a command into the intercom, and Robbins appeared obediently, casting an interrogative look at Julia's legs as he departed. "Don't mind Robbins," Penn-Wyant grimaced. "He's going through a hound phase just lately."

Julia shrugged indifferently and studied the hand on the envelope—definitely Aunt Lettie's distinctive, curly penmanship. The postmark was Tadbleak, an hour's drive north of London, which would make it two hours from St Martin's. Julia asked if she might read the manuscript.

Penn-Wyant assented, looked at her gold watch pendant, which looked like a miniature on her expansive bosom, and excused herself to go to lunch. Julia opened the envelope and began to read the manuscript.

CHAPTER 2

MURDER AFTER TEA-TIME
CHARACTERS

MISS RED GRIMSBY—attractive older woman, on the brink of fame for her brilliant sleuthing.

MISS BEATRICE LEASTWORTHY—her girlhood chum, gone a bit astringent in her old age. She doesn't approve of humans, but dotes on canines.

SIR ALFRED LEASTWORTHY—Beatrice's brother, the famous electronics wizard millionaire, who doesn't know when to retire.

Sir Alfred's two sons and their families:

ROLLO—the eldest. A squatty, retired fertilizer salesman.
CANDY—his young wife, who's no better than she should be.

J.G.—a steely-eyed capitalist, he manages his father's electronics firm.
JANE—his rabbity invalid wife.
OWEN—their punky adolescent son.

Sir Alfred's three children and their families: 22 see .. above

" " daughter a her family, perhaps:

MIRANDA POINSETTA—a fine-figured woman in her late forties with an eye for composition and the gardener.
GILES—her husband, a notorious soak and ne'er-do-well.
SCOTT—their oldest son, a fussy Communist accountant.
HARRY—their other son, a porno Adonis.

O'REILLY—the gardener, right from the pages of D. H. Lawrence.

MRS CLOVES—Sir Alfred's loyal secretary of twenty years.

TEDDY WINEAPPLE—Sir Alfred's young lab assistant, who is never privy to Sir Alfred's secret developments.

PLUS an assortment of servants and a policeman or two.

MURDER AFTER TEA-TIME

MISS RED GRIMSBY alighted sprightfully from her gleaming black Humber estate wagon and grimaced at the angry sputter of a motorcycle echoing eerily across the magnificent woods of Echo Wells.

Everything echoed at Echo Wells—something to do with the limestone escarpments behind the house. The cacophony of Sir Alfred Leastworthy's motorcycle had echoed across the park every day for the past thirty years, except for an occasional respite when machine or rider wasn't in good working order. People said Sir Alfred had a mania for his machine, as some have for their horses. Even now, at a ripe old age of seventy-two, when most men would have been nodding contently by the fire, Sir Alfred was still dead keen on leaning his bike over to the pegs, his grey locks flying in the wind, as he did the ton (whatever that was exactly, Red had never been quite clear).

Of course, Sir Alfred was no ordinary sort of chap. He had been born a bank accountant's son and now owned the bank. He had singlehandedly amassed a respectable fortune in the electronics industry when it had boomed after the war, and had gained a title in the process.

It was typical of Red Grimsby, a handsome, acute sort of woman who didn't look a day over forty-eight, to have all this information at her disposal, even though she had never met the man. She had a long-term acquaintance with Miss Beatrice Leastworthy, the great man's maiden sister, who had lived at Echo Wells since the demise of Sir Alfred's wife some fifteen years before. In fact, Red Grimsby's arrival was in response to an urgent summons from Beatrice, which had been scribbled in a spidery hand on the back of a Brighton dog-show program and delivered by Red's very own scottie, Tim.

Red had been absorbed in the judging of the Sealyham terrier bitches when Tim had slipped from her side. He returned just moments later, jumped into her lap, and dropped the damp message into her hand. As soon as Red had perused the note, she eagerly scoured the bleachers to catch sight of her cryptic correspondent, only to finally notice Beatrice looking entreatingly up at her from the row immediately below.

"Why, Beatrice Leastworthy!" Red gasped. But Miss Leastworthy put her finger to her lips and curtly shook her head. The blue-ribbon Sealyham bitch was about to be announced.

Thus, here was Red two days later, smartly attired in crimson wool, carrying one piece of <u>carmen</u> leather luggage and Tim in a matching travelling case, mounting the grey marble steps of Leastworthy's great house. She rang the bell. The door opened and Tim growled at the old butler who looked, quite properly, like a tortoise.

He showed them into the morning room—a nondescript sort of place in pale olive tones with good-quality blond teak furniture and thick brocade drapes in opalescent beige. The effect was restful, but barren of knickknacks. While waiting in strange rooms, Red often amused herself by considering what elfin touches would enliven the decor. At these times she wistfully wondered if she'd missed her calling as an interior decorator—but there hadn't existed such an occupation when she was young, and now the sort who had inundated the field insured that no one took it very seriously.

After she had added a fountain, festooned the modest mantel with plaster bagatelles, and opened the room's horizons with those delightful gold-veined mirror panels, she went to the window to redesign the garden. Outside, a wiry, swarthy little man in green coveralls was riding a power mower in ever-tightening circles. His heavy brow met irrevocably on the bridge of his nose, lending an animal intensity to his visage —an effect she found interesting. Her keen brain strained to recall what this figure reminded her of—certainly not her father—no, some literary figure . . . or perhaps someone out of an illustrated garden catalogue.

"Thank heaven you're here!" Beatrice Leastworthy, appearing in the doorway, exclaimed heartily—too heartily for a woman, really. She gratefully clasped the detective's scarlet-gloved hands. Tim demanded his freedom in piercing yaps until Beatrice scooped him out of his cage and hugged him, wriggling, to her bosom.

Red smiled indulgently and wished that Beatrice wouldn't wear her hair so short. Especially now that it was grey, it could have done with a bit more styling and a nice blue rinse, like Red herself used. And really, a large woman like Beatrice should take more care with her clothes—something more feminine with some ruffles would be an improvement.

"It's a pleasure to see dear little Tim, but where is the noble Rex?" Beatrice wanted to know.

"In his travelling case in my Humber. I didn't want to let him out just yet. A terrier like Tim is no bother, but a dog of Rex's size can be a nuisance to strangers."

"Nonsense! He's welcome! I've always admired Great Danes!"

"I appreciate that, but I doubt that the rest of the family will feel the same. It would probably be best to keep him in the kennel."

Beatrice nodded, saying that she'd instructed the gardener to prepare the kennel that morning. They settled on the divan with Tim between them. "Such luck running into you at Brighton! I don't get to as many shows as I once did."

Red clucked sympathetically. Beatrice had always been keen on dogs—nothing else, really.

Beatrice went on to rue that she didn't even keep a bitch anymore. "My brother doesn't like dogs—one of his worst failings. But I've refused to let him force me to give up Sparky. You remember Sparky."

"Dear old Sparky," Red exclaimed, unable to recall if Sparky was a dachsy or a spaniel of some sort.

"Five blues—and if that ruffian from Purley hadn't been judging—we'd have captured best of show at Hampstead in sixty-seven."

Red made more sympathetic sounds, hoping that Sparky wasn't one of those dreadful dachshunds who had lost its figure and waddled around labouriously on little wrinkly flippers like some sort of mutated seal.

"He's outside taking his exercise just now. He goes walkie two times a day—exercise is so important, even for an aging dog. And, of course, I worm him twice a year and keep a close watch on his stools."

"Very sensible."

Her friend went on a bit longer about dogs and their spoor before Red was able to change the subject. "But do tell me all about the family difficulties you mentioned in your note." Perhaps it was her sympathetic mouth, or the innocent—yet worldly—twinkle in her eye that made Red the sort of woman people confided in. Whatever the reason, Beatrice was soon launching into an emotional description of all the recent Leastworthy conflicts.

The family had never been an especially loving one. Beatrice blamed it on her brother's lack of interest. He had been fond of his wife in his way, but had never been a demonstrative man. He had spent the greatest part of his waking existence tinkering with gadgets in his laboratory. His motorcycle was his only diversion.

"Considering how little paternal interest he's taken in them, it's remarkable that his three children all live close by. Of course, J.G. is vice president of the corporation, so it was convenient for him to build his house on the west border of the estate."

"J.G. is the eldest son?"

"No, the second son, a year younger than Rollo. Rollo never got involved in electronics. He's spent the last twenty years roaming the globe—a salesman for a fertilizer company. He came back here and retired just six months ago with his new wife, Candy, which was a great shock to us all."

"J.G. and Rollo are your brother's only sons?"

Beatrice nodded. "And Miranda is Alfred's only daughter.

She lives in the second-floor apartment of this house with her husband, Giles Poinsetta. At the moment Harry, one of their two sons, is living there as well."

"How many grandchildren are there?"

"Only five. J.G. has one son, Owen. The Poinsettas have two sons, Harry and Scott. They also have two daughters—neither of which is living in England—not that I blame them, the parents they have!"

"The Poinsettas aren't model parents, then?"

"Not unless you call an unbalanced woman who's obsessed with sex, and her alcoholic husband, model parents."

"Oh dear!"

"And I daresay the sins of the parents have been visited on the sons. Harry makes his living—if you want to call it that—in London. Inherited his mother's interests—only puts them on film. She puts them on canvas. Just wait until you see the rude things she paints!"

"Deplorable!" Red gasped.

"I told Harry I wouldn't be surprised if he died of venereal disease before he reaches thirty."

Red winced at such careless disregard for euphemisms. Upon recovering her aplomb, she inquired about the other Poinsetta boy.

"Scott is an accountant."

"That's a nice, respectable occupation."

"Only he's pink. And this country's politics haven't deteriorated to the point where Communists are as respectable as you and I," Beatrice declared, her nostrils quivering in disgust.

Red patted her hand in commiseration and said that it must be so difficult for the family.

"I don't mind telling you, it is. And, as if that weren't enough, Owen—J.G.'s only child—just nineteen years old and already a drug abuser! I told Owen if he persists in smoking that poison, he'll be in an institution before he's thirty."

"How dreadful for his parents."

"Of course J.G. was livid. And his wife, Jane, who—God

knows—has enough health problems already, was so distraught when I told her that her son was on drugs, that she's had to go on tranquillizers! I felt it my duty to inform my brother—he is the head of the family, after all; but he would show more interest if we were robots, I'm sure."

Red nodded knowingly, for she had known a few men of Sir Alfred's ilk, and had never trusted them, although she accepted their necessary role in technical progress. They reminded her a little of foreigners—never really like the rest of us, even if they could speak the language.

"Alfred was outraged, as you might expect. Then that horrid affair between his daughter and the groundskeeper sent him right over the edge."

"Miranda and that creature on the mower? Oh my!" Red breathed, jumping up and staring out the window at the man who had now stopped mowing and sat on his machine, moodily smoking an unfiltered cigarette and staring at the ground.

"His name's O'Reilly—common as dirt, of course."

"Of course."

"As I was saying, my brother became hysterical. He called the family a pack of degenerate, unscrupulous vipers closing in for his death. He even threatened to disinherit us all and leave everything to his motorcycle mechanic. J.G. was quite right to inform him that such a radical change of his will at this point could be contested as senility. That was the straw that broke the camel's back. The next day Sir Alfred hired a private inquiry agent."

"To what purpose?"

"To gather filth. He wanted proof to support him when he disinherited the family as moral degenerates."

Red left her post at the window and returned to her friend's side. Tim, by now snoring, had rolled on his back. Frowning, Beatrice was abstractedly examining his stomach for fleas.

"The detective unearthed something questionable about Rollo's first wife's death. She fell from a cliff in Spain last year. They'd always fought like Kilkenny cats. And he'd been seen about with a dreadfully common woman—fifteen years his

17

junior, and no better than she should be. The first Mrs Rollo had her unfortunate accident, and two months later he married this young woman. He spent all of his savings on an extravagant honeymoon tour, then brought her back to live at the Beeches—his cottage on the northwest side of Echo Wells. The Spanish police couldn't discredit Rollo or Candy's alibis; but everyone knows what the foreign police are."

Sir Alfred's detective, with the instincts of a hound and the tenacity of a bulldog, had also ferreted out the cause of Giles Poinsetta's falling out with his business partner three years previously—tampered books, and Giles had been the culprit.

"Then there has been a mounting tension between J.G. and his father over the business. J.G.'s pushing some production changes that Alfred opposes. Alfred has always jealously guarded his ability to invent—a genius which J.G. has never had. And, I suppose, J.G. resents this. He has been pressuring Alfred to retire, which finally brought on a filthy row. J.G. called his father a paranoid old misanthrope. Alfred called J.G. a greedy vulture picking at a still-breathing carcass. Of course, it's true there's nothing J.G. loves more than money, but he's quite right that seventy is well past the time to retire ... I know I ought to keep out of it, but I must speak my mind. I told my brother that he's much too old to be riding a motorcycle, and that he should have retired ten years ago. He told me to shut up or get out." Beatrice dabbed at the corner of her eyes with her sleeve and fell into a miserable silence. The motor started up again outside, leveling to a steady whine, like a thousand locusts.

Red sighed and thanked her lucky stars that she had such a nice, ordinary sort of family. Aloud she commiserated, but admitted she couldn't see how she personally could ameliorate the situation. But Beatrice Leastworthy, who was nothing if not headstrong, would not take a negative answer. She implored Red to ask around a bit, to find witnesses unrelated to the family who would testify to Sir Alfred's shaky mental state.

"You're assuming he hasn't actually changed his will yet."

"J.G. has a spy in my brother's solicitor's office who will inform us the moment Alfred asks them to prepare a new will."

"There are other solicitors."

"That's why we've no time to shilly-shally."

"But what you require is testimony from a medical man. I doubt that a lay opinion would further your case."

"My brother refuses to see a psychiatrist—a sure sign of derangement, don't you think?"

"But surely there are ways to have a doctor observe him without him suspecting—at his club?"

"He doesn't have a club. He doesn't socialize or even drink at a pub. He spends practically every waking hour in his private lab at the plant. And he's become overly suspicious lately. Miranda says he really is paranoid."

And who could blame him, Red thought. She didn't feel the least inclined to get involved, and tactfully said as much. But, after a relentless round of persuasion and demurral, she reluctantly agreed to stay a few days and observe the situation before she absolutely refused to commit herself.

Ah well, two nights at the local inn might be pleasant, if the beds were firm and the food digestible. Besides, her curiosity was piqued—the grandsons alone promised to be interesting —a porno star, a Communist accountant, and a drug addict! If only Beatrice hadn't named them—it might be an amusing exercise to guess everyone's vice by the way they buttered their bread.

The two women strolled outside. Red released Rex from his travelling case. The huge Dane bounded and danced, while Tim tore along behind, yapping indignantly as he tried to keep up. Sparky, a watery-eyed old spaniel, immediately assumed a submissive posture when he spotted the giant hound.

Red dutifully fussed over Sparky, who seemed a bit deaf, while Beatrice rhapsodized over Rex. "So noble! Like some creature who stepped out of a medieval tapestry!"

"Those were whippets, I think," Red gently corrected.

"I see you use a closed carrier instead of an open wire cage —isn't that too stuffy?"

"Not in the winter. I find he gets overexcited when he can see everything—and his bark is deafening at close range."

Beatrice then summed up her years of experience with various parasite remedies as they installed Rex in the kennel, one of the several small buildings behind the great house. Red finally got away with a promise to return for dinner to meet some of the family.

The village, situated eight miles west of Echo Wells, hadn't much to offer in the way of architectural interest. It had a few dozen grey stone structures that obviously had comprised the original village. The two-story inn, which was one of the oldest buildings, stood beside a charming, ebullient stream, complete with a curved bridge. Red and Tim took a small but comfortable room and then had a leisurely tea, followed by a walk along the village green. Across the green from the inn and shops, an enterprising capitalist had built a hundred unattractive modern houses, each on a postage-stamp lot, without an ounce of individual charm or redeeming aesthetic value. Beyond them was the main road, which was lined with supermarkets and a dozen large industrial buildings. Leastworthy Electronics was, by far, the handsomest establishment on the street, thanks to the tall poplars, which disguised its typical warehouse lines. Red stood contemplating the plant for several moments, thinking what odd ways men had of accumulating fortunes.

Dinner with the Leastworthys was a memorable, if awkward, affair. Sir Alfred sat at the head of the table, never taking his eyes from the technical journal beside his plate. Red studied him curiously. She was impressed by the fact that, in spite of his frail appearance, he radiated vitality and concentration.

The old man's refusal to acknowledge anyone's presence seemed to intensify the undercurrent of tension in the room. No one addressed him directly, for fear of the inevitable snub, but everyone periodically glanced nervously in his direction. In spite of Sir Alfred's obviously peculiar behavior, the rest of the company felt constrained to behave civilly for the guest's benefit; but their efforts quickly disintegrated with the main course.

Red surreptitiously studied Giles Poinsetta, who had the unmistakably defensive air of an embittered failure. He was tall, fifty, paunchy, with a fringe of ginger hair and a hairpiece so shiny that it inspired an almost irrepressible urge to inquire, "Is that a new toupee?" His florid face had no doubt been handsome before it had acquired a habitual expression of truculent inebriation.

When Red politely inquired about his line of work, Poinsetta scowled and mumbled, "I'm in importing—and not a bad line of work until the wogs invaded. Not to mention the bleedin' Arabs! It takes all a white man's time just to keep his foot in the door these days."

"Most unfortunate," Red murmured.

"It's got nothing to do with luck, dear lady, it's a damnable conspiracy of foreigners and filthy Com—"

"Don't you ever leave off?" his son Scott snapped from across the table, clutching his fork like a weapon he'd love to use.

"Better stuff a sock in it, Pops," Harry, his other son, chimed in offhandedly. "Nobody wants to sit through your old comedy routine again."

Poinsetta glared from one son to the other and bellowed, "As I was sayin' before this pair of ungrateful jackanapes butted in, our own government is overrun with Bolshies who are sellin' us—"

"Giles, dear," Miranda, his wife, wearily began, "it's so typical of you to confuse your hostility against the world with your hostility against your sons." This peculiar statement had the immediate effect of taking the starch out of Poinsetta.

"All right," he muttered and tossed back his gin, groaning

as he clinked the glass loudly against his dentures. It was obvious that he had had a skinful already.

"That's the way, drink yourself to death," Beatrice grimaced.

Red glanced at Sir Alfred, but the old man showed no sign of having heard a word of what had just transpired. J.G. and his wife Jane (in her <u>wheelchair</u> by his side) both looked mutely pained. Their son, Owen, a pale, spotty-faced adolescent, didn't bother to conceal a spiteful leer.

Red then turned her attention to Miranda Poinsetta, who didn't appear the least bit ruffled by the unseemly altercation between her husband and sons. Was she indifferent or just inured? Whatever her nature, she was a splendid-looking woman in her late forties. Her large hazel eyes, milky skin, and full figure were enviable, but Red thought her dyed blue-black Grecian curls in poor taste, not to mention the peculiar long black artist's smock she wore.

"What's your line, Miss Grimsby?" Miranda inquired in her husky voice.

"Now that women's liberation is back in the news, I feel quite fashionable saying that I had a long career as a private secretary until I recently retired," Red replied, careful not to reveal that she was now free to devote her full attention to detection, which had always been her first love.

"Being a housewife, I can't help envying a woman who's found her niche in the world of men. I suppose it's my identity problem."

Red thought that really Miranda Poinsetta had probably found quite a niche for herself in the world of men, but said, "I've always considered raising a family an extremely challenging career." Perhaps too challenging, she thought, considering the two Poinsetta lads. Scott, the reputed Communist, with rosy cheeks and a bump of a chin, looked like a slightly hostile cherub of twenty-seven. His dark hair was already thinning at the temples. He was slight of build and round-shouldered, but had his mother's wonderful eyes, although his were presently glaring sulkily from behind his gold-rimmed spectacles.

Tall like his father, ginger-haired and well-formed, his younger brother Harry had won the family genes pool. Red would have mistaken him for just another beautiful athletic young man without a thought in his head, and would never have suspected the lurid aspects of the boy's athletics. It was rather a disappointment that there was nothing in his demeanor to suggest exhibitionist tendencies. Red had hoped for an excess of thick black body hair—or at least a tendency to never completely close the lips. It was always unsettling to know the worst about someone and notice that they appeared to be just like the rest of us . . . perhaps it was significant that he consumed vast quantities of food with noisy gusto.

"Harry, if you don't chew your food more thoroughly, you'll give yourself a bleeding ulcer," Beatrice admonished.

Harry, ignoring his great-aunt's advice, reached for the gravy. "Pass along that bream, thank you. And I'll just polish off that last chop, if that's all right with everybody."

Meanwhile at the other end of the table, Owen was having technical difficulties with the peas. Mistrustfully eyeing the serving spoon, he had painstakingly scooped up a ladle of peas, but spilled most of them on the tablecloth. They rolled away, it seemed to him, like thousands of miniature billiard balls. Giggling, he carefully avoided his parents' stony glares.

"What's the trouble, O., my lad? Met your match with those peas?" Harry winked broadly.

All eyes glanced nervously from Harry to Owen to J.G. to the old man.

"That is sufficient, Harry," J.G. warned icily, fixing his nephew with a withering look; but Harry didn't wither.

"Now, Daddy," Owen snickered, "be nice to Harry. He's a famous film star. Do a scene from your recent film success, Harry. We'd all love to see it—especially the ladies."

Harry was the only one who failed to react to this attack. Beatrice snorted indignantly. Jane squeaked and sank weakly back into her wheelchair. Miranda rolled her eyes and coughed on her cigarette, as J.G. rose ominously from his chair, leaning menacingly across the table as if to strangle his only son. But Owen's nasty smile never altered. They hate each other like poison, Red thought.

Harry casually blotted his perfect, <u>manly</u> lips on the back of his hand and said, "Better can it, O. You've gotten yourself too stoned to eat with the straight people."

J.G.'s jaw muscles began to twitch, as his effort to control himself was tested to the limit.

"Shut up, Harry," Giles mumbled. "Damnable, this is," he added to the empty glass he cradled mournfully in his hands.

"Why the hell should he shut up?" Scott demanded stridently. "Harry spoke the truth, after all," and pointing at Owen, "That snide little bourgeois twit is always higher than a kite! A perfect example of a decadent, effete, unproductive, parasitic—"

His mother wearily interrupted, "Scottie, why must you always interpret psychological problems as political problems?"

At that moment J.G. took a step towards Scott, but stopped, then took a step towards his own son, obviously torn between an overwhelming desire to simultaneously thrash his son and nephews. For a few tense moments, Red held her breath and waited for the entire family to exchange frenzied blows. But suddenly Sir Alfred, without a glance at anyone, grabbed his journal, rose, and left the room. As the dining-room door slammed behind him, expletives exploded from every lip. "Damn you Harry—you started it!" "I've had it with the bloody lot!" "There's no excuse—" Only Red remained sitting quietly, feeling as if she were at one of those dreadful modern plays about the psychological reality of family life— namely, how much they all would thoroughly enjoy murdering each other.

Red slipped quietly from the room and asked the butler, who was carefully polishing the doorknob to the dining room, to have someone bring her motor round from the garage.

"I'll have O'Reilly take care of it for you, madam," he replied, reluctantly abandoning his post. Every word of the continuing fracas could be plainly heard in the hall.

The butler returned, helped Red into her smart Astrakhan coat and escorted her to the front portico. In the drive, her Humber gleamed in the moonlight. O'Reilly touched his cap and gave her a hand into the driver's seat. She thanked him.

"That's what I'm here for," he replied. His voice was a wonderful soft purr.

"And you manage the gardening as well."

"Aye. And keep after the pheasants."

Red beamed into his brutish face. Here was someone who knew how to muck out a stable and any number of other rough and ready activities. He seemed somehow a creature out of date—a link in man's evolution before underarm deodorants and office jobs were invented. She speculated about what it would be like living with such a creature as she drove down the long, curving drive.

The next morning dawned brisk and fine. The air smelled of woodsmoke and leafmold as Tim trotted ahead of Red along the trail that led to the abandoned quarry east of Echo Wells. The terrier caught scent of rabbits and frantically tugged at his leash until Red indulgently freed him. Barking excitedly, he dashed ahead, as his mistress, careful not to turn an ankle, continued her unhurried descent.

A spattering of stones clattered past her, one catching her painfully on the shoulder. She nervously glanced back up the trail in time to see a huge stone tumbling down the quarry wall towards her. Crying out, she swerved from its path of destruction not a moment too soon. The stone crashed by, causing the earth to shake beneath her feet as it careened and bounced down to the quarry floor.

Red sank gratefully to her knees when it smashed well clear of Tim and his rabbit hole. She felt dizzy. Her heart pounded in her throat. It had been a near miss from what would surely have been a fatal accident.

But had it been an accident at all? Red uneasily peered up the trail, but gorse and bracken obscured her view. A few pebbles rained down. In Red's experience, boulders didn't just happen to fall on people—they were pushed. Her breath came in rapid gasps as she looked for a place to hide.

CHAPTER 3

JULIA THOUGHTFULLY TURNED the last page of the manuscript. On the back of the page was a scribbled note from Lettie. "Dear Mrs Penn-Wyant. I am not at all satisfied with the names of the characters. Please change them for me—you're so much better at that sort of thing that I am.—L.W."

What a peculiar sort of note! Lettie had often bragged to Julia that part of her trademark was choosing good names for characters. And why did the old girl insist upon using that tired old stone-pushed-from-above routine again? Better motor right up to Tadbleak and find her immediately. It was remotely possible that this manuscript was too close to a real situation for comfort. It didn't seem at all impossible that someone who had read enough of Lettie's books might be inspired to actually attempt to flatten the old girl with a boulder.

Julia hurried through the throngs of workers returning from their lunch hour. She felt like breaking into a song-and-dance routine as she realized that she was not going to spend the entire afternoon in the office.

Although she'd intended to be on the M1 North in half an hour, she was unable to get away before three. There were too many papers on her desk that had to be shuffled before her manager would hear of her leaving early. She protested, the words "I quit" on the tip of her tongue, but only said that her family problem was of some urgency. Julia finally agreed to type up a half-dozen pages of flack before grabbing her coat and heading for the door.

By the time she had gone home and packed a few clothes into an overnight bag and thrown them in the boot, the afternoon was beginning to fade. Still, feeling like a child on the last day of the term, she impulsively put the convertible top down, bundled up in a wool coat, hat, and scarf, and was off.

Well ahead of the rush hour, she managed to reach Tadbleak after an hour's fast drive. She stopped for petrol and inquired of the attendant if he knew of an estate nearby that was remarkable for an echo.

"That would be Callingwoods, the Lechwood estate," he replied and directed her to take the turnoff west of the village and drive six miles beyond the long stone bridge.

As she continued on her way, she passed a stone inn called the Dreadful Boar; it closely resembled the one described in Lettie's manuscript. She parked in front and went inside. The lobby was dark walnut, with glowing amber coach lights and too much black leather furniture. The landlady was dusting her collection of scenic plates on the shelves behind the desk. Julia quickly learned that Lettie was indeed a guest there, but that the landlady hadn't seen her since she'd gone out that morning.

"She hasn't been around here much, has friends in the area, I gather. She went out late last night and I didn't hear her come in, but I did see her leave again early this morning."

Julia went up the dark stairs, carpeted in a rug depicting a bucolic scene of cows and cottages. She avoided stepping on the cows. A knock on Lettie's door got no answer. There appeared to be nothing for it but to crash the gates of Callingwoods.

The lane to Callingwoods wound through a forest severely beautiful in the fast-fading twilight. The bare limbs made scribbled black lines against a luminous purple sky. Although her cheeks burned with the cold, Julia couldn't bring herself to put the top of her roadster up and shut out the delicious night.

Just past a typical Stockbroker's Tudor, she spied the twin pillars the attendant had told her marked the entrance to Callingwoods. She geared down and turned amid the towering wall of evergreens that lined the drive, cutting off what little light remained. She took in another deep breath of crisp piney air and vividly felt the perfection of the moment. It was good to be alone and in motion, gliding through a serene, motionless world.

But then the serene world of black silhouettes distorted into a half-glimpsed horror huddled by the road. Despite the acuity of her senses, the shape at the fringe of her headlamps was there and gone before she could comprehend it. She had only enough time to veer to the right before she was past. As she swerved to avoid running off the pavement, her hat was jerked from her head, which was odd, since it had stayed in place during the faster part of the trip.

The Austin crashed gently into the thick boughs of a pine and came to a softly cushioned stop. In her sudden rush of adrenaline, the silence seemed to fall upon her like a great blanket. There were no lights visible anywhere, save a dim glow from the Austin's headlamps buried in the fronds.

She nervously turned in the seat and peered back into the night. A fallen deer? A human body? Something was back there in the dark, lying motionless in a black stain.

"Get a grip on yourself, girl. Wouldn't it be smart to drive up to the house and come back with help? Yes, that sounds wonderfully sensible." Agreeing with herself, she engaged the starter, and her sports car responded true to form. Grind Grind. "Damned traitorous bucket of bolts. Up to that nasty little game again, are you?"

After a few tries the panel lights dimmed—now the battery was too low. Cursing, she rummaged for a torch, found it, clicked it on; but nothing happened. "Blast." She hadn't remembered to buy new cells to replace the worn-out ones.

Which was the most appealing course to follow? Hiking up a dark lane, heart in throat, listening for God-knows-what to work the same foul business on her as it had to whatever was lying back there? Or stumbling around in the dark trying to ascertain exactly what it was and what had been done to it? Or sitting in the car until dawn, waiting and wondering?

"None of the above," she said aloud, getting out of her car and walking gingerly back towards the Thing in the Road.

(was this not choosing "B" above?)

Something thin and cold suddenly sprang against her chest. She flinched, suppressing a scream. To her gloved hands it felt like piano wire, obviously taut—it twanged when she plucked it.

Ducking under, she realized that here was the reason for her hat's sudden disappearance. Hollywood violence scenes flashed through her head as the tip of her shoe hit something soft, yet firm. She reflexively jumped back, slipping in a puddle of thick stuff, and putting out her gloved hand to avoid falling. The hand came up wet and cold, the wool soaked through. The urge to throw the glove away was irresistible; but as she pulled it off, the odor that filled her nostrils was oil.

Carefully exploring the Thing in the Road with her hands, she was relieved to discover it was neither man nor beast, but motorcycle. The padded seat was the terrible soft thing that had given her foot such a turn. Again her hand was sticky. The machine was obviously leaking profusely. She absent-mindedly wiped her hand on her jeans, all the while considering the inescapable implications of a wire strung neck height for someone riding a motorcycle. Horrified by the grotesque image of inadvertently kicking someone's head like a football, she fell into the dreamy, cold paralysis of a complete funk. Her heart pounded. The pine needles whispered. Her hair blew into her face. The dark night turned a little blacker still.

After an eternity of several seconds, a low growl joined her pulse and the wind. A pie shape of the darkness was sliced away as the growl resolved itself into the sound of an auto coming in the gate. The headlamps stopped a few feet from her. Julia shielded her eyes. The car door opened. A tall, bony man unfolded himself.

"What's the problem?" he called in an American accent.

She balanced on the balls of her feet, ready to dash for the trees, should he come any closer. The situation suddenly vividly struck her with an obvious truth that had never even occurred to her before. Men were formidable enemies, since most of them were bigger and stronger. This had never been a problem she had had to face until this moment. As the initial nauseating impact of this realization subsided, she experienced a surprisingly cheerful firmness of purpose and self-confidence.

"I'm Julia Carlisle."

"Woody Baxter." He held out his hand.

"We'd better not shake, unless you want a handful of oil. Are you related to the Lechwoods?"

"No. Are you?"

She shook her head. "Look, something awful—I think—has happened. I was just in the process of trying to discover—" She abruptly abandoned the effort to explain what she didn't comprehend, in favor of surveying the scene in the light. There was no doubt, now, that the puddle under the wire was blood. But there was no body evident in the island of light. "Oh God," she groaned, unable to take her eyes off the brown, sticky mess.

"What is it?" He was suddenly at her side. She quickly moved beyond his reach. For a moment they silently surveyed each other in the glare of the headlamps. He had an odd sort of face—not unpleasantly simian with little dark eyes and deep grooves from his rather flat nose to the corners of his broad mouth. His disheveled hair was shoulder length. She guessed his age at thirty or so.

"I'll get my flashlight," he said. She watched him go to his car, half expecting him to return brandishing a snub-nosed revolver. Being an American, she thought, he was probably always armed to the teeth anyway.

Lovely, it was just a flashlight. He flashed it along the perimeter of the trees, then crouched down over the motorcycle. "This motorcycle has been shot."

"This is no time for humour."

"You're telling me. Here's a bullet hole, which explains the oil . . ." He trailed off, messing up his hair a little more. "Sonovabitch!" he suddenly cried. "This is an antique Flying Squirrel—this is Sir Alfred Lechwood's bike!"

"I was afraid of that."

"Go up to the house and call the police," he ordered.

"And what will *you* be doing in the meantime?" she demanded.

"Looking for the body—obviously."

She considered the situation for a moment. How did she know he wasn't just returning to the scene of the crime to pick up some bit of incriminating evidence? "No. I'm sorry, but I haven't the vaguest clue who you are or what you're doing here. And I'm not at all certain what has happened here. My instincts are to stay put and keep a lookout. *You* go call the police."

"We have the same instincts. I guess that makes it a stalemate."

"We could both go, but someone might come along. Any car higher than mine would tear the wire right away from the tree. In fact, that's what you would have done, if I hadn't stopped you."

"I'm getting tired of that fishy look. Are you some kind of detective, or something?"

"No, I'm a copywriter. And you?"

"I'm a boy-wonder electronics freak. But let's get acquainted later. You win, I'll go call the fuzz. Be careful." He handed her his torch. His running footsteps faded into the distance.

Suddenly she was aware of being alone. The trees and darkness were perfect cover for a lurking sniper. And here she was, the perfect target, neatly outlined in Baxter's headlamps. Shivering, Julia began a painstaking search for the motorcycle's rider.

From the west, the rustle of someone coming swiftly through the fallen leaves brought her up short. She backed into the shadows and waited silently.

"What are you doing there?" a woman's husky voice called. Julia turned on the torch and directed it on a short, attractive woman with a mass of black curls. She was wearing high boots and a long black cape, right off a gothic cover.

"Get that damned thing out of my eyes. Who are you? What are you doing here?"

"Let me ask you the same question," Julia replied.

"Of all the cheek! I live here!"

Of course! Right out of Lettie's manuscript! "Are you Sir Alfred's daughter?"

"That's right. Miranda Poindexter. Now who are you?"

Julia introduced herself as Lettie's niece and confirmed the assumption that Lettie had, indeed, been a guest at Callingwoods. As tactfully as possible she advised Mrs Poindexter of the bizarre circumstances that had set her fumbling through the umbrage.

Visibly alarmed, Mrs Poindexter insisted that they resume searching. They clawed through the pines, moving the boughs to shine the torch on the ground beneath. "This is the working of a pathological mind," she uttered, more to herself than to Julia. "Who could have done this? Who could have done this?"

"Steady now, hope for the best—we don't know the worst."

"I was painting all afternoon," Miranda said. "Every time I reached for a tube of colour it was black . . . I hadn't intended to use so much black. I was uneasy, but I thought it was because of Sparky's poisoning. Beatrice blamed it on Father, of course. I've always known that she hated and resented his success—a deep-seated sibling rivalry, with sexual undertones, of course. She never married, you know. I'm certain she's still virginal at her age. That's not good for the psyche, I don't care what anybody says."

"What were you doing walking across the park in the dark?" Julia inquired.

"What? I said I was painting, didn't I? I suddenly looked up and noticed it was getting dark. I knew I had to get back before Giles got home from the office."

"Where are your paints?"

"I left them in the cottage . . ." She tripped over a root and screamed, grabbing Julia's arm. It was a moment before she found her voice again. "We might even stumble over him— talk about trauma!" Her hysterical laughter turned into a sob.

"Father!" She shouted it several more times; the echo had a weird, mocking quality.

Henry Treece's lines drifted into Julia's head: "The wood is full of shining eyes, the wood is full of tiny cries. You must not go to the wood at night."

Another car turned into the drive. Julia dashed out and flagged it down. A familiar tiny figure alighted.

"Julia!"

"Auntie!" Julia cried, giving her a hug and gratefully inhaling the familiar smell of Rosemilk and mothballs. "I was so worried about you!"

"I'm sorry, dear. What has happened here?"

Julia quickly explained. Lettie took it all in quietly, including Mrs Poindexter, who was shivering violently, obviously in the process of coming unglued. "I'd best take this poor woman up to the house. She'll catch a chill." Lettie led Miranda away out of the range of the headlights. Soon afterwards, a torch bobbed swiftly towards her, coming from the direction of the house.

"Police and ambulance will be here in a few minutes," Baxter panted. "Found him yet?"

"No. I've covered every inch from here back to the wire. No more blood or anything that I saw."

They continued the search. Needles scratched Julia's face, but she barely felt them, her skin numbed from cold. She glanced at her watch. It was five forty-five, only twenty minutes since she'd turned into the drive, but it seemed she'd been groping in the dark for hours.

"Here comes a car, probably the police. I'll flag him down."

A tall, middle-aged man got out of his car. He had a lot of ginger hair that looked too stiff to be real, and a handsome face that had gone to wattles. Gin lingered on his breath. Julia guessed that he was Giles Poindexter, Miranda's husband, coming home from the office.

At first he couldn't seem to take it all in. "But what's the gen?" he asked several times, staring from Julia to Baxter in blank bewilderment, as they tried to make him understand. "What are you doing here? I don't like it."

Julia drew Baxter aside and asked sotto voce, "What *are* you doing here?"

"I came to see Sir Alfred, of course."

"Was he expecting you?"

"Not exactly. He knew I was coming sometime this month, but I had originally expected to be here a few weeks from now."

"What were you coming to see him about?"

"Lighten up on me, honey. That's none of your business," the American said lightly. "I could ask you the same questions, you know."

"I came to see my Aunt Lettie. She's here—uh—visiting the family."

"But you don't know any of them yourself?"

Julia shook her head.

"So has the old fossil finally snuffed it?" Giles asked over Julia's shoulder. "You can tell me. Has he really cashed it in at last?"

Neither of them responded. Baxter visibly stiffened, then looked away in distaste. Julia stared at Poindexter, amazed at his callousness.

"Well? Where is he then?" Giles wanted to know.

"We don't know," Julia replied evenly. "We don't know what happened—and won't—until we find him."

Poindexter considered this carefully for several minutes, swaying slightly from side to side. Then he shook himself like a wet dog and straightened his shoulders. "I'll have to break it to the little wife very very gently. She was fond of her old man, in spite of everything. You wouldn't guess it, but she's not a stable woman. Too much psychology. Too much artiness. It's turned her outlook all arsy-tarsy."

They were spared the necessity of a reply by the noisy arrival of a cadre of police cars and the ambulance. Grim men began setting up floodlights, their bodies flitting across the beams of their headlamps like moths about a flame. A dark shape, hunched over in heavy overcoat and hat, approached them. Outlined from behind by the lights, he touched a hand to the brim of his dew-rimmed hat and addressed them.

"Good evening. I'm Constable Jones. You, sir, are Mr Baxter?" The American nodded. "Very good. I've a few quick questions . . ." but he was interrupted by one of his men summoning him to answer a call on the car radio.

"I hope to hell they find him," Julia whispered to Baxter, suddenly aware of tension gnawing at her stomach, as she looked into his anxious face. "Did you—I mean—do you know Sir Alfred personally?"

Baxter regretfully shook his head. "Only by reputation, but I'd have gladly genuflected and licked his boots."

The constable returned. Time began to behave normally again. The scene lost a little of its nightmarish quality as the dozen men went to work. Julia felt better, somehow, describing what had happened, as if telling normalized it. The constable listened attentively, jotting a few notes in a little book.

After Giles and Baxter had also been briefly questioned, they were all escorted to the house. Giles went straight up to his second-floor apartment. Baxter and Julia were shown into the morning room. Baxter paced like a caged lion. Julia collapsed into a chair in front of the fire, removed her shoes and slowly rubbed her frozen feet. Then an officer appeared and asked the American to "Come this way please." Baxter followed him out the door.

Lettie appeared.

"However did you find . . ." she asked, taking a chair beside her niece.

"The postmark on the manuscript. Look here," Julia scolded, "have you taken leave of your senses? If you let that magazine publish *Murder After Tea-Time,* and the Lechwoods get wind of it, they could sue you for every shilling."

Lettie colored guiltily. "Do you really suppose they'd ever see it? Oh, I was reluctant, borrowing so directly from life! But I needed a plot and here it was! It was so . . ."

"It won't seem so easy when their solicitors get through with you."

"Would anyone be so brutal as to sue a harmless little old . . ."

"You know as well as I do that you're not harmless."

Lettie blushed again and dithered apologetically, but Julia continued sternly, "Furthermore, it was most unkind of you to disappear like that."

"I thought if no one knew I was here, it would keep people from connecting the story with the Lechwoods. The editor will change the names and everything will be . . ."

"Well, you've given the Brighton cousins another dozen grey hairs, not to mention myself and your housekeeper! You should phone them immediately and let them know you're safe and sound!"

Lettie acquiesced and Julia abandoned her scolding tone for a brisk one. "Best put me in the picture immediately. Someone didn't actually attempt to squash you with a stone, did they?"

"Of course not, dear, who would do such a thing?!"

"So you just couldn't resist using that old cliché one more time."

"What cliché? Dear, I make it a point to avoid clichés like the plague."

"But the situation is otherwise as you described it in your manuscript?"

Lettie nodded. "With developments."

For a moment the two were silent. "What do you think happened out there tonight?" Lettie finally asked in a quavering voice.

Julia shrugged grimly and said, "Start at the beginning."

Lettie prefaced her narrative by disclosing that she had known Beatrice and her brother Alfred when they were at school together, but had lost touch a few years after their school days ended. She had now and again encountered Beatrice at dog shows, but hadn't seen Sir Alfred for fifty years. Lettie stared into the fire for a moment, gathering her thoughts before she launched into a narrative which, she wistfully commented, would have made an excellent second installment of *Murder After Tea-Time*.

Only yesterday evening (the ninth of November) Sir Alfred, true to habit, got a pint paper carton of milk tonic from the kitchen and retired to his study to drink it. He had taken up this health drink routine ten years previously, and only recently had ever complained of any health problems—an occasional headache and leg pains. Beatrice had urged him to consult a physician, but Sir Alfred had refused, remarking that he had lost all faith in physicians when he was a medic during the war. His sister warned him that if he didn't calm down he'd have a stroke; which, typical of her advice, had the immediate effect of sending him into an apoplectic rage.

Yesterday evening his first sip of tonic seemed to taste odd. Assuming that the milk had turned, he tore the top of the carton away and gave the contents to the spaniel, who was lying by the door. Sparky promptly lapped it up and lay down on the hearth rug. Sir Alfred threw the carton into the fire and finished reading the paper. When he got up an hour later to go to bed, the dog was dead.

"Poison! They're trying to poison me!" he bellowed. The butler (the only live-in servant) came running, as well as Beatrice and the Poindexters. When they burst into the study, Sir Alfred rushed past them and locked himself in his bedroom, refusing to let anyone in, in spite of repeated entreaties.

Meanwhile, Beatrice was prostrate with grief over the body of her beloved pet. The hysterical woman told the butler that her brother was insane and that he had deliberately poisoned the tonic to kill her dog. She ordered the butler to summon Lettie from the inn at once.

By the time Lettie had arrived, the entire household was in an uproar. Rollo and J.G., who had also been summoned, were at their father's locked door, alternately begging him to listen to reason and threatening him in vague innuendos if he didn't open up. Lettie finally persuaded the agitated Beatrice to down some brandy and go to bed. The other family members present (Harry, his parents, J.G., and Rollo) were badly shaken and obviously suspicious of one another.

"Who had the opportunity to poison the drink?" Julia asked.

"Anyone in the family, really. The kitchen staff works from eleven a.m. to eight p.m. At any other time, it would be a simple matter, under the pretext of fixing a cup of tea or fetching an ale, to tamper with the cartons of tonic on the bottom shelf of the fridge."

"What about visitors other than family members?"

"There weren't any in the past few weeks except myself."

"Not a sociable family."

Lettie, agreeing that it was an accurate observation, continued. "As soon as I arrived last evening, I suggested calling the police; but they would have none of it. J.G. insisted there was some reasonable explanation for the 'unfortunate accident' that had befallen Sparky. I finally gave up, contenting myself to spending the night in Beatrice's room, just in . . . "

"Did you see Sir Alfred this morning?"

"Yes. I was in the kitchen at seven thirty when he came in, looking very distraught indeed. Apparently he'd refused to talk to anyone in the family at all, although Miranda had tried reasoning with him. He wouldn't speak to me, but put the remaining dozen cartons (I'd counted them immediately upon my arrival the night before) of health drink into a sack and roared off on that machine . . . " She trailed off and peered up at the American, who had just returned and sprawled into a chair. He looked thoroughly disheveled and worried.

"They wanted to know what I was doing here. I told them, but they didn't seem to like it. What a night! I got bad vibes as soon as I drove into this place," he said grimly.

"I know what you mean," Julia nodded.

"If he drove straight into the wire, he could have been decapitated," Baxter grimaced. Lettie closed her eyes, and said nothing.

"I thought of that. Out there . . . I was afraid of finding him like that," Julia admitted quietly, "but after a while, when I didn't find the body, I thought something else might have happened—since his body should have been near the wire if he had been decapitated . . ."

"But if he was only wounded and managed to somehow survive," Baxter suggested, "he could have wandered off someplace and fallen down unconscious."

"Or someone could have come and taken his body away," Julia guessed.

They sat in weary silence, listening to the footsteps coming and going in the hall and the quiet, indistinct words of policemen conferring. Then a young constable looked in and told them they could leave for the night, as the driveway was clear.

"Have you found him?" Baxter and Julia chorused.

The constable shook his head. "Reinforcements have just arrived. We'll comb every inch of the county until we find him."

Lettie remained to look after Beatrice. There was no one in the hall as they left. The police had started Julia's car for her. It sat beside Baxter's in front of the porch. She couldn't help peering into the trees on the way out of the park. The wire was gone. The ambulance remained. The powerful klieg lights still illuminated the entire area as several men worked over the motorcycle. She could see ghostly figures moving through the trees, as the mist began to settle in. The moistened branches of the trees, heavy in the evening stillness, caught glints of light, flashing out of the forest's darkness like watching eyes. Julia was very glad indeed to leave Callingwood's gates.

to stay where for the night?

CHAPTER 4

IN THE MORNING SUNLIGHT the scene had lost most of the bizarre quality of the night before. The ambulance and police were no longer in evidence, and the motorcycle had been taken away by the time Julia arrived on the grounds once more. She crossed a small arching stone bridge over a rushing stream, turned several curves, and caught sight of the house. She parked by the front door, just behind a new black sedan. It was momentarily unsettling to hear what sounded like a dozen departing sports cars, until she realized it was the echo of her own Austin, growing fainter and fainter. She hadn't noticed the effect the night before when the police had driven her up.

"Uncanny," she said, alighting and looking about at the immense expanse of wooded park. The house was an uninspired three-story yellow brick box, with a great many windows and chimneys. As she stood looking at the building, the great red front door opened and a man emerged, frowning and staring abstractedly at his feet. He came down the steps two at a time. She cleared her throat, or he would have surely walked into her.

He stopped abruptly, regarding her with keen grey eyes behind large aviator-style spectacles. He looked a tense sort of person—not much older than thirty-five, which would make him too young to be J.G. Lechwood. His face was long, his moustache a bushy reddish brown beneath a prominent nose. He had a neat head of thick wavy dark hair with flecks of grey.

Julia considered his ultracorrect three-piece grey striped suit and quipped, before she could prevent herself, "You're too well-dressed and brainy looking to be the gardener."

"I'm flattered." He bowed slightly, his voice was low.

41

"You have the athletic build, but the ever-so-slightly re-pressed air rules out the skin flicks."

"Oh well, *that's* not so flattering. It's not at all fashionable to be repressed, is it?" His pronunciation was overprecise.

"Not unless you're discussing your hangups with every-body—"

"And boring people blue with a lot of psychological cod's wallop—"

"And frankly soliciting lots of body contact with absolutely everybody you encounter," she added. He chuckled. "But, if you aren't the bloody capitalist or the earthy gardener, or the porno grandson, who are you?"

"I should think it would be obvious—I'm Edmond Darian, the dashing inspector from Scotland Yard—called in from London, you know."

"Oh, hell, I've put my foot in it, haven't I? One shouldn't wax whimsical with Scotland Yard."

"Only if one can manage it with such panache—Miss?"

"Julia Carlisle."

They shook hands. "Ah yes—the first one on the scene last night."

"Have you found him?"

He frowned and answered in the negative.

"How peculiar. What *have* you found out?"

He consulted his watch. "I'm so sorry, I have an urgent appointment." He bowed slightly and moved away.

"You're not the forthright sort, are you?" she called after him.

He paused and turned, an official deadpan on his face. "Forthright sorts make excellent witnesses, but inadequate detectives. A pleasure meeting you, Miss Carlisle." He nod-ded, got into his sedan and purred away.

The butler showed her into the morning room and went away to find Miss Winterbottom. Julia was staring out the window at the gardener when a young Greek god with a mass of woolly ginger hair sauntered in.

"Sorry, didn't know anyone was in here," he said, absent-mindedly flexing his biceps that bulged under a green-and-gold rugby shirt. He wore yellow silk track shorts that show-cased a pair of excellent legs. "I was looking for my squash ball."

"Squash in those threads?"

He glanced down, as if to check what, if anything, he was wearing. Our porno star, Julia silently surmised.

"I'm not going to play squash. I squeeze the ball, develops the grip."

Julia said this was news to her and introduced herself.

"Harry Poindexter."

Julia murmured something about deja vu and pretended to search her memory for where she had seen him before. He eagerly suggested that she'd probably seen him in one of the earliest significant alienated little films—*If Only.* "I was one of the school boys who gets machine-gunned down in the Quad."

"Of course! The one in the blue athletic shorts!" she ex-claimed, amazed that she really had recognized those legs! There had been a long shot of them at the end, drenched in blood and bits of ivy-covered wall.

"Right you are," he grinned, leaning against the mantel and crossing one leg across the other knee. *GOOD TRICK!*

"Been in other films?"

"Dozens. But that was the only straight one. I'm still trying to break into the big time. Meanwhile I'm making ends meet in the pornos." He shrugged philosophically.

"That's a kinky line. What's it like?"

"Like anything else, I guess—with its ups and downs, but not without perks, if you know what I mean."

"I can imagine."

"Smashing for the old libido, as Mother would say. Need some bread? I could get you in my next film. You've got a nice pouty look, and the straight, angular haircut—you could do the French maid with Lesbian tendencies."

"I already have a job, thank you. And my French isn't con-vincing."

"It's not your French that has to be convincing," he smirked, searching through the drawers of the escritoire by the window. "You were the first one to come across the wire last night, weren't you?"

"Yes. You all must be terribly worried."

He closed a drawer and appraised her for a moment. "You're damned right we're worried. Nobody would have minded awfully if old Alf had a nice innocent spill and dropped quietly off the hooks in a ditch somewhere. The solicitor would slice the pie and everything would be roses. I keep asking myself why the slimy bastard who's responsible didn't just stage some subtle accidental-looking show instead of this absurd wire routine? The other thing I keep asking myself is what the hell happened to the old man's body?"

"You really are disgustingly cold-blooded, aren't you?" she remarked, but thinking that he had made some salient points, indeed.

"I suppose I am, but you'd better appreciate me, since I'm one of the finer human beings you'll encounter here. Trying times bring out true colours, they say, speaking of which, poor Scott is beside himself with the trembles."

"Scott—your older brother?"

"The one and only. The Yard has found out that he's pink. But that doesn't absolutely prove he's an assassin. So he's pink—how else can the poor clot prove his bleedin' manhood? I just hope he doesn't go into a funk and make a balls of it."

"What blunder is he likely to commit? Confess?"

"Even Scott isn't that thick. If any of us cracks under the strain it will probably be to tear Aunt Beatrice's hair out. She went and nobbled to the cops that she thinks Candy killed Alf. Uncle Rollo turned purple when he got wind of it."

"Candy is—"

"Married Uncle Rolly Polly because she thought he had money. So the family hates her like poison. So what else would she marry the ass for? But that doesn't mean she done in old Alf."

Just then Lettie appeared, and Harry made a hasty exit.

"I just noticed that boy has a cleft chin—a sure sign of a warm, affectionate, passionate . . ."

"Spare me the Oriental physiognomy lessons. You look tired. Did Beatrice keep you awake all night?" Julia asked, checking the hall for eavesdroppers. Satisfied that no one was about, she carefully latched the door.

"Oh my, yes. She went on for hours about her brother insanely murdering her only dog. She got into a state about insanity running in the family. When I finally got her quieted down she had nightmares. I got very little . . ."

"Poor pet. You really should go back to the inn and get some rest."

"I know, but being here in the thick of things is the best way to glean information. I've been very busy this morning!" She then informed Julia of the details on how Sir Alfred had spent the previous day. On the way to work he had left the remaining cartons of health drink at the chem lab down the road from Lechwood Electronics. He arrived at the plant only a few minutes late, and worked in his lab, as usual, until lunch time. He ate a shepherd's pie at the Thistle, where he always lunched. "Then, contrary to routine, he stopped at J.G.'s home."

"You don't say! We must find out what transpired!"

"J.G. wasn't home of course, he always dines at his club. His wife Jane was apparently who Sir Alfred saw." Sir Alfred then returned to work and, true to habit, returned home for tea at four; but, locking himself in his bedroom, refused to take food or drink.

"I wonder why he bothered to go home for tea at all, since he didn't take any—for fear of poison, I assume."

Lettie gave her an admiring smile. "Julia, you're a natural for this sort . . . but, perhaps he came home out of habit. We are all creatures of . . ."

"Mmm. Go on."

"Shortly after four, a local man had driven up to the servants' entrance with a load of firewood. He stacked the logs beside the kitchen door and drove back down the drive at twenty past four, noticing nothing unusual and nobody in the park."

"But he wouldn't, if they were lurking in the pines—they're a veritable fortress," Julia remarked, uneasily remembering the black wall of trees.

"At four-forty, Sir Alfred left the house to get back to the lab, in order to work until dinnertime, as he always did. Both the butler and the cook noticed the noise his cycle made as he drove off, but no one claims to have actually seen him leave. Cook thought she heard a backfire soon after that."

"The bullet in the tank?"

"Probably. The bits of hair on the wire matched those in Sir Alfred's comb. The blood was type O—the same as Sir Alfred's—and millions of others."

"And the thin trail of oil?"

"Motorcycle oil. It starts several hundred yards from the house and . . ."

"Which marks fairly closely at what point the shot hit the bike," Julia deduced.

"I expect so."

"Any spots where there's a larger concentration of oil?"

"Just right before the wire there's a bit more."

"On the house side of the wire?"

"Yes."

"That's very interesting."

"Why, dear?" Lettie asked, but Julia didn't seem to hear her. She gazed out the window, chewing her lip for some moments.

She finally said, "The trees obstruct the last half of the driveway from the house. Is that also true of the second floor and attic?"

Lettie said it was. They sat with their private thoughts; Julia abstractedly watched Lettie twiddle her thumbs and wondered in what century B.C. thumb-twiddling was discovered. Were there thumb-twiddling figures on the walls of the pyramids? Perhaps it was an evolutionary step towards weaving and knitting?

"What about the health-food drink he left for analysis?"

"Uncontaminated. Quite a surprise, but then . . ."

"The police are doing an autopsy on the dog, of course."

"Yes. That's about all I . . ."

"I'm impressed. How you could have gleaned so much information by—" She looked at her watch. "Nine a.m. is a wonder."

Her aunt blushed with pride. "Thank you, dear. I guess I've got the . . ."

Julia agreed that she certainly did and asked what her next step would be.

"Gossip with the cook. Do come along."

"How shall I gracefully barge into all of this?"

"Not to worry. I've told everyone you used to be an operative with an inquiry agency in London, and that you're totally reliable, of course."

"Lettie! I never—"

"Just a white lie, dear, an indispensible tool . . ." Lettie's blue eyes twinkled gaily.

"You shock me! I never realized before how positively immoral you are."

"Neither had I, and now it's rather late to capitalize on the . . ."

The entry hall was teak-panelled with a collection of heavy antique mirrors and a magnificent bannistered staircase that led up to the Poindexters' apartments. The kitchen was at the back of the house to the right of the hall. They found Cook and the maid, Smith, reading a lurid film magazine at the kitchen table. They needed little persuasion to gossip.

"The butler informed me that you heard Sir Alfred leave yesterday after tea."

The cook, who looked remarkably like a famous wrestler from Liverpool, took a deep drag from her cigarette and said, "That's right. I was outside that door, getting a snort of fresh

47

air. I'd burned the pie and it had smelled up the kitchen so. There's nothing reeks like burnt flour—exceptin' feathers, of course, that's worse yet. And there I was, and I heard his motorcycle. The air was chilly and I thought it wouldn't do the old boy any good to have his naked head out in the cold—him being already upset about Sparky and all. I knew he'd catch his death—"

Smith gasped.

"I didn't mean that—oh, you know."

"Miss Beatrice was clean off her nut about that dog dying, she was," Smith said.

"It had a face only a mother could love," Cook chortled, then lapsed into a smoker's cough.

"Didn't it slobber so! And that snotty nose!"

Julia asked if any of them had heard anything interesting that might shed some light on what had happened.

"You heard something interesting yesterday, didn't you Smithy?" the cook cackled obscenely, dropping her cigarette butt on the floor and stamping it out.

"That I did. I was pushing the carpet sweeper along the hall rug on the second floor—it was round about half past."

"Half past what?"

"Four. I heard voices coming from Harry Poindexter's room. It was his voice and a woman. At first there was just giggles. Then I heard him say in a fakey Cockney: ''ullo, where'd you git this lovely refined scar?' And she says 'go on wicha!' Then there's a sound like a slap and he roars in a grand voice, 'then crown my joys, or cure my pain, give me more love or more disdain.' And she says, 'oh, you know, can you?' That's the limit, ennit?"

"Oh my!" Lettie gasped. The cook laughed lewdly.

But was the maid certain that it was Harry's voice? Smith was quite certain.

"Did you recognize the other voice?"

Smith shook her head. "At first I thought it was Candy Lechwood. I'd heard them go a round of slap and tickle over the billiard table once. But it wasn't her. I couldn't say who it was." She hadn't heard anything after that, as she had to go down and help Cook start dinner. "I looked at the clock when I came down and saw it was just a few minutes before five. I thought: I hope Cook's peeled the pratties already."

The conversation then turned to the relationship between Miranda Poindexter and the gardener. Cook was convinced that they were having a bit on the side and that Sir Alfred should have sent the scoundrel packing the minute he got wind of it.

"Oh no!" Smith cried, hands on broad hips, eyes flashing. "O'Reilly told me himself that he could never—you know—with a woman that talked like that. And I believe the man."

"Because it suits you," the cook muttered cynically.

Reddening, Smith rallied to his defense. "O'Reilly's a good man and no one can deny it! Hasn't he always been so particular about the herbaceous borders? And what about the pheasants? Doesn't he fuss over 'em like a mother hen?"

"I did hear him go on to Sir Alfred the day Sparky dug under the fence and killed one of them," Cook admitted. "He came up to the house carrying what was left of the bird, blood dripping down his trousers, tears running down his cheeks. It was a terrible sight."

At that moment the man in question entered. The smell of pine and damp earth and manure blew in with him. He was humming what could only be an ancient Celtic ballad.

"I'm for me breakfast," he told the cook, blinking indifferently at the rest of them, as he made his way to the sink where he rolled up his sleeves to his elbows, and then slowly lathered up his hands and arms. He rinsed them carefully in cold water, thoroughly drying them on a towel.

"Your dustin' needs tendin' to," Cook reminded Smith, who, like Lettie and Julia, watched, fascinated by O'Reilly's deliberate ablutions. The maid glared at the cook and left the kitchen in a huff.

O'Reilly sat down at the table, stuffed a napkin into the open neck of his rough green woollen shirt, and poised knife in one fist, fork in the other. Cook placed a huge plate of kidneys, brains, and assorted other entrails in front of him. "Is there any fried bread?" he asked.

"Keep your knickers on."

Lettie cheerfully requested that he answer a few questions, to which he replied that he couldn't talk and eat at the same time, and began putting his breakfast away. Reluctant to watch him devour the unappetizing-looking mess, Julia retreated to the outside, Lettie close behind. She was latching the door behind them when a tall, scarlet-faced man with a sagging middle stumbled into the kitchen from the hall.

"It's Giles Poindexter!" Lettie whispered. They both peered through the crack.

Poindexter was scowling and mumbling belligerently, "There you are, you scum," as he swayed slightly over O'-Reilly.

"Can he really be sloshed at this hour?!" Julia wondered.

"He's in a shocking mood, that's obvious."

"You filthy lying bugger!" Poindexter bellowed, clutching for O'Reilly's throat. Cook screamed. O'Reilly attempted to sidestep the assault, but Giles caught him by the shoulder and dragged the table to the floor with them. Giles' hairpiece sprung from his head and—like something the cat had dragged in—skittered across the floor. The two combatants grunted and struggled, Giles clumsily attacking, but obviously no match for the gardener, who fended him off easily.

"I'll never let you take her—I'll kill you first!" Poindexter gasped, writhing ineffectually as O'Reilly pinned him to the floor amid the brains and entrails that were spattered everywhere.

"I don't want her, you drunken fool!" the gardener growled.

"I'll cut your bloody—"

"You'll shut your gob before I lose hold of myself and cripple you," O'Reilly warned, at which point Poindexter ceased to struggle and began to retch. The gardener jumped up and lunged for the door, charging past Julia and her aunt.

"I underestimated that man," Lettie remarked. "He deported himself . . ."

"Like a gentleman," Julia furnished automatically, and then added after a moment, "You know, we really must follow up this alibi of Harry's. Did anyone see the girl leave?"

"I don't know, but I'll see what I can find out. Let's walk around a bit."

There were a half dozen small buildings behind the house, and a garage, and a hundred yards behind that, a rectangle of rough earth that had obviously been a vegetable garden. Beside the garden stood the potting and implement shed, then the pheasant enclosure and kennel. All were painted white with green trim and looked in excellent repair.

"What's off that way?" Julia was pointing across the lawn to the north.

"The Beeches is over there—a half mile or so, behind that rise. It's a grand name for Rollo's little cottage. It's nothing compared to J.G.'s house, and positively minute compared to this . . ." She gestured towards the great house behind them.

"Imposing pile."

They tramped round the side of the house and down the drive. It was a fine morning—the sun was unseasonably warm. Only the falling leaves made it seem like November.

"I wonder if the police found any telltale bits of clothing or dropped matches," Julia mused, poking among the leaves.

"I wouldn't know. But what good would it do them if they had? I eschew that sort of clue in my books—they don't prove anything except that someone dropped them there in the last month. It doesn't necessarily put the clue dropper there at the time of the crime."

"True. What's that way?" Julia pointed to their left, which was west.

"Nothing much. The rude cottage where O'Reilly lives, a quarry that's inoperative these days, a bog, then the lane joins up with the high road north. Apparently the lane is rarely used to get to the highroad, or the Little Dorpling Station—it's much quicker through the village."

"How far is the train station?"

"Twenty miles."

"And O'Reilly's cottage?"

"A mile."

"That's the direction Miranda came from last night."

"I see. Oh dear, perhaps, after all . . ."

"Mmm."

"Let's go this direction." Lettie headed eastward. "J.G.'s house is just over there."

"Close by the Callingwoods pillars. I noticed it as I drove up."

Lettie said they should have a chat with J.G.'s wife. "I hope the master of the house isn't in. He's a steely-eyed tyrant, and no mistake. Jane is a rabbity sort of creature—no chin to speak of—in a wheelchair, you know. She fell off a horse, quite a while ago I believe, and has made a hobby of her ailments ever since—at least that's what the rest of the family . . ."

"Not an overly sympathetic lot, are they?"

J.G.'s house was a two-story affair with lots of ersatz wainscoting and thatch. A maid let them into the living room where Jane Lechwood sat embroidering by the fire. She seemed alarmed to see them, but it could have been just her normal expression—the bulging pale eyes. Her light hair was tucked into a wispy bun. She wore a shapeless grey wool dress that didn't suit her.

At first she seemed evasive and reluctant to discuss the previous day. Try as she would, Julia couldn't winkle any information out of her. Then Lettie took command of the situation, with positive results, to Julia's bemusement.

"You were flummoxed by your father-in-law's sudden visit yesterday, weren't you, dear? And who could blame you, he hadn't even spoken to anyone in the family for almost a fortnight—so awkward . . ."

Jane opened her mouth to speak, but resolutely closed it again.

"And here he was—at your door! It must have been a very difficult encounter," Lettie clucked.

The bait was irrestible. "It was maid's day off. I had just taken my injection of megavitamins when I heard the bell."

"And his manner was odd . . ." Lettie prodded patiently, her voice wise and reassuring.

"Very odd."

"What did he say to you? Did he actually accuse anyone of poison?"

"No. He—" But Jane caught herself and reluctantly closed her lips, pinning them with an incisor.

"Come, dear. Your husband doesn't want you to tell us about it, does he? But we know already, so it isn't as if you're letting the cat out of the bag, just the details. With your help we might get to the bottom of this dreadful business as quickly and discreetly as possible."

"You don't know about it, how could you?"

"From the rest of the family. Everyone's been most cooperative. So he asked you what you thought of the poisoning?" Lettie encouraged.

Jane's jaw dropped. "You do know! Well, since you know —" she was obviously dying to tell. "He said, 'Do you think they'll succeed in murdering me next time?' I tried to reason with him—that he was just imagining things, that there had to be a perfectly innocent explanation; but he wouldn't listen and soon left." She pulled a wrinkly handkerchief from the inside of her sleeve and dabbed at her eyes. "It gave me such a blinding headache."

"I shouldn't wonder!"

"Then that evening I heard the siren and my heart sank. Heart attack, I thought. I was afraid to call the house, but finally forced myself to dial the number. The butler answered. He didn't make much sense—something about Sir Alfred's motorcycle and that the police weren't letting anyone drive through. I called J.G. at the club immediately. He came right home."

Julia inquired how Owen responded to the situation.

Jane didn't answer, but looked doubtfully from one to the other.

"About the police—what was your son's reaction to the news that something was amiss?"

"We were alarmed, of course," the woman carefully replied. "But we thought it wise to sit tight and wait until J.G. returned—which was within the hour. By the time the police came to our house I was on the verge of nervous collapse. I took a sedative and went to bed." She went on, vaguely referring to a variety of grievances—her health, her husband's problems with his father, the family's immorality; she seemed to have finally exhausted the subject when she suddenly flushed and leaned forward in her wheelchair. "J.G. told me not to tell the police," she said, a confidential craftiness in her voice. "He wants to protect his sister's reputation. There's nothing wrong with that."

"Yes, I mean, no, of course not, go on, dear," Lettie prodded.

"I saw it with my own eyes—in the potting shed, Miranda and that common groundskeeper—rolling in the dirt like animals!" Her eyes dilated, her breasts heaved. "Smashing over pots and bags of fertilizer! Making low guttural cries! I couldn't bear to watch!" She paused to mop the perspiration above her lip, then concluded in triumphant disgust, "Their bodies were filthy with potting soil!"

"You saw this in the potting shed—with your own eyes?" Julia probed, watching her carefully.

"Yes. It was nauseating."

"No wheelchair could have gotten across the rough stretch of earth that surrounds the potting shed," Julia quietly remarked. Jane's flushed face paled, acquiring a mortified, watchful look. Julia debated if she ought to pursue this tactless tack or not.

Lettie murmured an excuse, and Julia followed her aunt's quick exit. "That was a bold—but perhaps an unwise stroke," Lettie remarked as they walked back to Callingwoods.

Julia grimaced. "I couldn't resist. I knew that she was lying or—"

"Or else she doesn't need that wheelchair."

"Exactly."

"Notice how her mouth frowns to one side? A sure sign of discontentment, say the Chinese."

They agreed to meet for tea and parted company—Lettie back to the house to work on an alibi list, and Julia to tour the park further.

CHAPTER 5

JULIA FOLLOWED THE SINUOUS ROUTE of the stream that spilled noisily over blue granite. Leaves floated like fairy boats in little pools around which mossy stones crouched like green furry animals.

In a small hollow a body stretched out on a flat rock in the sun—pale and slight, lying on his stomach, dangling his long hands in the icy water.

Julia called hullo and perched on an adjacent stone. He turned his head to reveal a long, narrow, blotchy adolescent face below a dreadful skinhead haircut that exposed a lumpy skull.

"Lovely spot you have," she said.

"And effing private until just recently. Who the bloody hell are you?"

She introduced herself. "And you're Owen Lechwood."

"Oh charming! Just what we need—another interfering bitch. Have you brought a pack of dogs with you too?"

"Don't be such an infant."

He sat up and glowered into her face. Judging that she had at least a ten-pound advantage, she waited eagerly for him to strike. But the moment passed. He shrugged out of his sweater and tee shirt and lay on his back, his palms upward, his eyes closed. His skin was extremely white, lined with prominent blue veins.

"Warm for this time of year."

"Go on. I'm thrilled to bits."

"You're an obnoxious little ass, aren't you?"

"Oh I beg your effing pardon." He sat up again and found a crooked joint in the pocket of his tight jeans. As he palmed his match, squinted, and lit up, he reminded her of the children that queued up in front of the Elephant and Castle cinema for the Saturday matinee: noisy, shabby, sexy, fag-smoking ten-year-olds, queued up for a Walt Disney flick.

Two streams of smoke billowed from his nostrils. "Fancy a quickie?"

It was several minutes before she could control her taunting laughter. He sat cross-legged, smoking, and watching her, an ugly smile on his face. There was once again a potential for violence between them. She fingered with satisfaction the three large rings on her right hand—excellent weapons.

He finished his joint and lit another, which spread a relaxed blank expression across his face. He reclined and closed his eyes. Considering him, Julia keenly felt the futility of getting at the truth from a few remarks that may or may not be intentionally misleading.

"It's this haircut, isn't it? It repulses you," he said with obvious satisfaction.

"Well, it isn't a turn-on, that's definite. Why'd you shave it? To offend everyone?"

"No—to get a job. I nearly got on as a roadie for the Sickies."

"*The* Sickies—the big punk rock group?"

"That's right. What browns me off is that their old roadie recovered from his knife fight sooner than expected. So I never got my chance. Just my effing luck."

"That is rough. The Sickies must be raking it in."

"Bloody right. They've got enough hostility going for them to make them an effing fortune."

"How'd you get in with them?"

"The drummer's an old friend of Candy's."

"Candy—your Uncle Rollo's wife?"

"You'd be surprised the friends that bit of goods has! The girl has excellent public relations. The only male that doesn't come on to Candy is dear old Daddy. But what do you expect from a man who sits in his office beating off on pound notes? What boggles is why a fluff like that married an old fart like my uncle."

"Do you loathe all your relatives?"

He took a long drag from his cigarette and tossed it into the stream. "Some more than others."

"What about your grandfather?"

"He wasn't on the top of my homicide list, if that's what you mean. Oh, I was fed up with him. He should have had the decency to snuff it years ago. We were all fed up with the old sod. Take his only sister, you should have heard her the night her dog croaked! She went up to his room and screamed at him through the door. Accused him of poisoning it, which he probably did, and threatened to get revenge. And what about my dear daddy? All he did was bitch and moan about Grandfather getting in his way at the plant, bad for business, too old to be productive, no concept of cash flow, on and on. He wanted him dead, all right."

"But would your father have done something so crude as string a wire across the road?"

"It doesn't sound like him." He squinted thoughtfully. "But he might take a shot at him and make it look like someone else did it. That's his style."

"I gather you're not overly fond of your father."

"You're quick, you are. Aunt Miranda says it's Oedipal—but that's a lot of cock. It's true, I would get a certain amount of pleasure out of standing triumphantly over Daddy's bloody corpse, but Mummy definitely isn't my type."

"What makes you despise your father so?"

"He's a pain in the ass, hypocritical bastard, for starters."

Julia tramped back towards the house, swinging around the back to confirm her first impression that the potting shed would be inaccessible to a wheelchair. The earth had been plowed, leaving big clumps of hard ground that would have been impossible to navigate on narrow wheels. She was going round the side of the shed when she overheard voices coming from inside. She stopped and listened, instantly recognizing Inspector Darian's precise tones and O'Reilly's deeper, slower response.

"How long has this been here?" Darian wanted to know.

"Ages, I'd say by the cobwebs. I had use for it last summer to get rid of some varmints. That's the last time I had cause to take notice of it."

A small mention of her rising and leaning would not be amiss here!

"Where was the level of poison when you last noticed it?"

"There, I reckon, can't be certain, though."

"Do you keep this building locked?"

"No reason to."

There was a pause. Hearing a footfall, Julia flattened herself against the side of the building.

"There you are," said O'Reilly. "Constable wants to ask you a question."

"Yessir," a young voice said.

Darian dismissed O'Reilly. Julia heard him leave the shed and start up the mower.

"You assist O'Reilly?"

"Yessir. I come on Saturdays and Tuesdays after school."

Darian asked the child the same question he had asked O'Reilly. The boy had apparently not taken much notice of the pesticide, but he thought it had been there a long time. He could be of no help in determining if the level of liquid had gone down recently. The inspector thanked the boy and told him he could go. Julia waited to hear the sound of Darian departing. He crossed the shed, but her heart sank when she realized that he was coming around the corner of the building. They were suddenly face to face. He looked startled, then annoyed. He folded his arms across his chest and regarded her inimically.

She shrugged and ruefully remarked, "There's nothing like getting caught spying to make one feel like the east end of a westbound cow."

"I don't approve of interfering females—not even attractive ones. In my line of work, they're a damned nuisance."

"More so than interfering males? Try to sound a little less chauvinistic." As she folded her arms in an unconscious mimic of his stance, she noticed that he wasn't much taller than herself.

"I would love to discuss sexual equality and other fissiparous subjects with you sometime, my dear girl, but right now I want to know what you were doing skulking around, eavesdropping on confidential police interviews."

"I've never heard anyone say 'fissiparous' before."

Muttering something she didn't catch, he led her around the building and into the potting shed, where he leaned against a wooden table and fiddled with his pipe. Watching him, she wondered if the pipe was a self-conscious prop. Pipe fiddling never failed to show the fiddler to an advantage—unlike cigarette rituals.

"Well?" His tone was brisk. "What were you doing out there?"

Feeling at a disadvantage without her own prop, she inspected her fingernails and replied that she wasn't lurking with the express purpose of eavesdropping, but impulsively took advantage of the opportunity to do so when she heard voices.

"I'd advise you to give up sleuthing—it's not a healthy hobby."

"Especially not for women, right? Do you recommend needlepoint or cake decorating?"

"Why are you being so tiresome?" He gave her a long look that she couldn't quite fathom.

"Because you're so supercilious, dammit. It puts my back up."

"I doubt if you're taking the risks seriously," he said finally. "I should hate to see you hurt." He puffed his pipe carefully for some moments. "I can't allow you to continue messing around in this business, for your own sake as well as mine."

"I shall be very careful. And I shan't interfere with your investigation. In fact, if you would leave off putting me off, I could be of help."

"No."

"Will you quit being so pigheaded and listen?" she began, and related to him Jane's story of the lurid scene she'd claimed to have witnessed. He listened politely. "But she couldn't have seen anything like it from a wheelchair. The earth is too rough all around. And she couldn't have seen all that from anywhere but through the window, or door at close range."

Darian stroked his moustache and looked around at the floor, then, grinning, looked up at her.

"And why," she laughed, "is old sour puss suddenly exhibiting his dental work in that artless fashion?"

"It just suddenly struck me as one of the perks of the job —a lovely woman telling me dirty stories."

"Aren't you lucky? Now it's your turn—find anything interesting on that bottle of arsenic?"

"Just evidence that it's been handled lately."

"And Beatrice's Sparky died of arsenic poisoning?"

"I'd rather not comment on that at this time."

"Spoken like a politician," she grumbled, crouching down to get a better look at the floor. The soft dirt was a confusion of indistinct prints. "I suppose your lab boys will sift through every bit of this now."

He crouched down beside her, letting some dirt sift through his fingers. He assured her in his most official manner, "If we find even a few molecules to substantiate Jane's dirty story—I promise you'll be the first to know."

"What a magnanimous gesture," she remarked, over her shoulder. The inspector was obviously an inconsistent beast, she thought, thrusting her hands into the pockets of her blazer as she walked away. He was a clam one moment—then let a little information slip the next. She had detected a subtle shift in his attitude somewhere between the description of low animal cries and rolling about in the dirt, smashing pots. At that point they had both glanced at the pot shards that littered the floor. Then their eyes had met in what Julia recognized as one of those long looks that crop up in books so often. Depending on the sort of book it was, it might not be too many more pages before the looks warmed up markedly.

CHAPTER 6

LETTIE WINTERBOTTOM found no comfort in her second cup of tea. What on earth could be keeping her niece? Of course, a clever girl like Julia could take care of herself, but this game had all the earmarks of danger . . . "All the Earmarks of Danger," that would make a lovely title. The ancient fertile imagination had her thoroughly alarmed by the time Julia arrived, looking as fit and impudent as ever.

"There you are at last—home . . ."

"Dry and on a pig's back. Sorry to be late." She pecked Lettie's rouged cheek and slid into the booth beside her. "I came across Owen—there's a nasty bit of work."

Lettie said he was an impertinent little monkey.

"Has he got a decent alibi for the afternoon in question?"

"His mother is his only alibi."

"Wouldn't you know. Anything on Harry's lurid lady?"

"No one saw her enter or leave the house. But she could have slipped down the back stairs, out the back door, and walked across the park towards town—where she might have left an auto."

"She might have seen something important. Draw me a map of likely places she could have left a vehicle."

While Lettie sketched a rough map, the waitress came with scones and strawberry jam.

"What about the alibis of the rest of our suspects?"

Lettie handed her a list on the back of a knitting pattern for an overly cabled sweater:

Sir Alfred heard leaving the garage on motorcycle at 4:40. Julia discovered wire at 5:15.
Alibis:
Giles Poindexter—two business associates are alibi. Had drink with them at office. Left them at 5:30. Arrived Callingwoods soon after. Ahead of police.

Miranda Poindexter—no alibi. Claims was painting alone in O'Reilly's cottage because there is "an excellent view of the quarry from there." Claims saw no one from 4 to 5:30.

O'Reilly—no alibi. Says was hunting voles near the bog. Saw no one. Was home when police called at 6:30. Four freshly killed voles were in evidence.

Harry Poindexter—unnamed girl is alibi. Overheard in bedroom by maid at 4:35. At first insisted was alone in room, but when confronted by police with maid's evidence said "I'll never reveal the lady's name." The butler says that Harry was alone in room when he summoned him at 5:35.

"Did the butler look under the bed or in the closet?" Julia inquired, looking up from the list.

"Probably not."

"Humph." She resumed reading:

Scott Poindexter—dentist in Tadbleak is alibi. Left his accounting office early—3 p.m.—to keep dental appointment. Left dentist's at 5:15. Arrived home according to landlady at 6 p.m.

"Scott is an accountant for the north county chapter of the Labour Party. He resides in a dreary flat in Tadbleak. His landlady lives below him."

"The Labour Party, very interesting. Is the dentist's office forty-five minutes from Scott's flat? How did he spend that time?"

Lettie said she didn't have that information yet.

Julia went over the remaining suspects:

J.G.—he and secretary left office, as usual, just before 4. J.G. claims went directly to his club, where his wife called him before 6 p.m. Witnesses corroborate that he was at club.

Jane—maid's day off. Son Owen is alibi.

Owen—mother is alibi. They were supposedly at home alone together from 4 on.

"But we already know that Jane Lechwood is a liar."

"Nobody lies or tells the truth all the time."

Only Rollo, Candy, and Beatrice remained.

> *Rollo*—his wife is only alibi. Claims at home with her all afternoon. Both home at Beeches when police arrived.
>
> *Candy*—husband is only alibi.
>
> *Beatrice*—no alibi. Says drove her car to Marmsley Close—25 miles north. Seen leaving house at 3 p.m. Claims she saw no one who could give her an alibi. Parked in secluded spot and walked. Returned home 6:45 p.m.

"Oh yes, there's one person I forgot to include. Sir Alfred's motorcycle mechanic—several customers and one assistant were with him all afternoon at the garage until five-thirty."

"Once again you've acquired a wealth of information in a very short time, Auntie! I don't know how you do it!"

"Relentless prying, dear. You know, this case reminds me of the *Hot Buttered Rum Murders*."

"It's rum enough, I'll grant you."

"There are just too many mutual alibis—and lack of alibis."

Julia ticked them off on her fingers. "Miranda, O'Reilly, Jane and son Owen, Rollo and wife Candy, and Beatrice. I suppose they have to be our chief suspects for the moment— all with a variation of the same apparent motive—impatience for inheritance. Except O'Reilly."

"But if he really is having an affair with Mrs. Poindexter . . ."

"He might be plotting to lure Miranda and her inheritance away from her husband? O'Reilly hardly seems the type."

"Perhaps it's her idea."

"It won't wash, somehow. This whole inheritance motive is all wet, especially when you look at the blatancy of the method —an attempted poisoning, a shot, a wire—all sheer madness for someone eager for the inheritance. As Harry said, a murderer with any smarts would have constructed an accidental-looking trap. That would have ensured a quick signing of the death certificate and a quick reading of the will."

"Mmm—I have a feeling that the shot and the poison are the keys to this case—not the wire."

"Whatever do you mean?" Julia looked at her sharply. Was the old girl lapsing into one of her vague fits?

Lettie lowered her eyes to the task of pouring tea. "I can't explain it, I just have an intuition that we should concentrate on the poison and the shot," she insisted stubbornly.

Baffled, Julia let it pass. "Then what is your feeling about the reason for Sir Alfred's mysterious visit to Jane Lechwood? *I* have a feeling if we knew why he went there, we'd know quite a lot."

"You always were a clever girl, Julia, even as an infant you were . . ."

"Don't you have an old friend who was very big in the foreign office?"

"Yes, the Colonel, retired now."

"But still with connections?" Lettie nodded. "Good, why don't you have him check up on the Rollos—his first wife's death in Spain—and anything he can get on Candy."

Lettie thought that was a capital idea. They paid their bill and left the tearoom. While Lettie wrote a wire to the Colonel, Julia purchased several dozen envelopes from the postmistress.

When Lettie inquired if she had a lot of correspondence, Julia shook her head, but wouldn't reveal what use she intended for the envelopes. Lettie was obviously slightly offended by her companion's lack of candor, but suffered in silence.

Heat radiated from the black cast-iron stove that squatted in the middle of the room. The stove was festooned with raised black scrollwork, looking like someone had filled a cake decorator with cow manure—a pastry cook's scatological fantasy. The effect was enhanced by the chrome fenders and a silvery trophy, complete with garlands.

Nothing else in the interior of the rude stone hut was even remotely whimsical. The furniture was sparse and old—one wooden table, two chairs; the sturdier one still wobbled as Julia sat in it. There was a sink and a bed with a dark wool patchwork quilt. Several rifles leaned against the wall in one corner.

"I probably breastfed the boys too long," Miranda said, squeezing a tube of chromium yellow onto her palette. She never took her eyes from the huge canvas leaning against the window that overlooked the quarry.

Julia had peeked at the canvas and made a faint comment about "interesting use of phallic imagery," in lieu of a more forthright reaction.

"But one never knows when mothering is really smothering."

"Do you paint here often?"

"Lately—yes. It's like the navel of the universe here—don't you feel it?" Miranda made a vaguely expansive gesture. "One feels that this rude hut just evolved. The rocks just rolled together into a pile."

"The place does have a certain elemental charm," Julia admitted, squinting her eyes to play the old childhood game of seeing animal shapes in the rocks—an elephant, a bird, a smiling Buddha.

"Like its master—the beast in his lair. He comes and goes all hours of the day and night. His door is never locked because he fears neither man nor beast."

"It would be rather nice—to not be afraid of anything."

Miranda quickly glanced at her. There was an unmistakable look of anxiety in the woman's remarkable hazel eyes. She looked tired and harried, still not recovered from the dreadful night before. Julia wondered what she could say to gain this woman's confidence, and was about to try a different tack, when O'Reilly blew in on a cold draft.

A furry rabbit corpse was draped over his shoulder, a rifle in his hand. He acknowledged Julia with indifference and avoided looking at Miranda at all. He carefully placed the weapon among its fellows, pausing for a moment, staring at the guns. He muttered something incoherent and pulled out a large knife. The handle was heavy, the blade long and bright. He removed a stone from the faded cigar box on the table and scraped the blade back and forth in slow, graceful strokes. "I told you to take your paints out of here," he said quietly, his eyes on the knife.

"Not until this canvas is completed."

The tension between them was obvious. There seemed a mutual wariness, but its nature was puzzling.

"This is no place for paints," he grumbled.

"You don't understand anything about it," she responded tartly.

The gardener grunted, returning the stone to the box. He slung the rabbit from his shoulder and into the sink, and proceeded to skin it. Miranda, an oddly intense expression on her face, moved closer to watch the procedure over his shoulder. She reached out and touched him. He shied as if stung.

"Look what you made me do!" he cried.

"Oh! You've cut your thumb!" She ripped the scarf from her hair and bound his wound with it.

"You made me ruin the pelt," he muttered.

Julia heard a car stop outside, footsteps, a heavy knocking.

Miranda continued wrapping his finger, as if in some sort of daze.

"Shall I get it?" Julia said, turning the knob. "Hullo, Inspector."

Darian's voice and manner contained the perfect British blend of polite authority. "Would you mind coming along with us, Mr O'Reilly?"

Miranda began to sob. "I know he didn't do it! I'll tell you the truth—we were together all that afternoon. Look—here's the proof—I was doing his portrait," she proclaimed, dramatically pointing to the canvas.

"My dear woman," Darian said, briefly considering her handiwork, "that could be anybody."

Scott lived in what was probably the only cold-water flat left in Tadbleak. His landlady, Mrs Crawly, a seedy woman of lumpy proportions in a shiny new Tesco house dress, let Julia into the smelly entryway.

"He ain't in from work yet. Any minute now, or not 'til late —it's one or t'other."

"Does he get in late a lot?"

"Are you his lady friend?" she asked, giving Julia the once-over.

"Her sister. I want to know what his intentions are. Poor Sissy is afraid he's seeing other women."

"Is she now?" The rheumy eyes lit up with interest. "Well, that's as may be, but he isn't bringing them here. He's out late three or four nights a week. Says it's political meetings. Is your sister one of them pinkos too?"

"No, indeed. And I feel confident that Sissy can reform Scott, once they're married."

"No use trying to change them, I say."

"I'll just go up and wait," Julia said, climbing the stairs, before the old girl had a chance to stop her.

"What did you say your sister's name was?" Crawly shouted up after her.

The flat was as spartan as O'Reilly's cottage, only drearier. A naked bulb illuminated the battered desk piled high with books on economics and scribbled notes. There was a dilapidated couch losing stuffing on the arms, and not so much as a radio in evidence.

"Good God, no wonder he never comes home."

She busied herself searching the desk. There was nothing but reams of notes in a cramped hand, none of which meant anything to her, as it was all in economicese. There was no personal correspondence, no telltale lavender-scented envelopes, no photos, no magazines, nothing of any human interest whatsoever.

There was a decent Brueghel reproduction tacked to the wall, as well as a Polish poster depicting a worker standing immense, mechanically godlike, atop a platform of tiny factories. The bathroom was decorated in 20s waterstains. Two towels of sinister Scandinavian geometric design hung across

68

the tub. There were several wafer-thin slivers of soap on the sink—the sort Julia would throw in the trash.

There were no interesting drugs in the medicine cabinet. Even his toothbrush was of the most modest, proletarian design. She thought it odd to be seeing it all in colour, when it was obviously a set for some gritty black-and-white *film noir* of Belgrade.

Scott wasn't pleased to find her there—it showed all over his pleasant, boyish face. "Excuse me. Did I interrupt your spying?" His voice was high, appropriate to his image of an aging kindergartener: a pugnacious cherub, in an inexpensive mud-coloured suit, carrying a briefcase and a copy of *The Times.*

Smiling disarmingly, she said that she had gotten bored waiting.

He stared fixedly at her shoulder, which made her wonder if he was on drugs, but then he said, "Excuse me, you have a loose thread on your blazer." He quickly snatched it away. She caught the faint scent of some familiar pleasant smell—not cologne. He gingerly deposited the offending thread in the trash and said, "Thank you."

She accepted his offer of tea and watched his tea ritual in fascination. It was a maddeningly fussy routine, involving a quirky tendency to converse with specks of lint found on the tea cloth. He instructed the kettle to boil and looked immensely gratified when it eventually did.

Handing her a cracked mug, he remarked, "I haven't made up my mind how I shall treat you," and laughed nervously. His laugh was a swallowed explosion, sounding like "oof." She said that she could understand his ambiguity. He removed his glasses and polished them carefully on his handkerchief, making a show of holding them up to the light, polishing, then holding them up to the light again to ensure every speck was removed.

"I just came from O'Reilly's cottage."

"Oh really?"

"Your mother was there."

"My mother is a fool," he fulminated. "Not that Pater isn't an ass—but there is no excuse for such decadent philandering —"

"Scotland Yard came and took O'Reilly away."

His eyebrows shot up. "No!"

"I don't know why, yet; but when they invited him along, your mother confessed that she had been with him all yesterday afternoon."

His face turned scarlet. "That was clever of her."

"I don't know if they believed her."

"I don't know that I would believe her either."

"Forgive my impertinence, but do you believe that she's really having an affair with him? I only ask because it strikes me as a little off somehow, now that I've seen them together."

"Mother and a common beetlecrusher, you mean? That's the appeal, I'm certain—something shocking. She's only doing it to wound. And it's very effective! The bitch! How could she do it?" he wailed, hugging his stomach pathetically. "Oh, it's not the class thing I mind—better a member of the proletariat than some bloody capitalist—it's just so tacky."

Julia recalled Miranda's remark about breastfeeding; perhaps she really had overdone it with this one. "You lead a very austere existence here," she murmured, glancing around.

"You find this alien? That's because you're bourgeois. A member of the bourgeoisie is nothing without his material goods around him. The Party, of course, does not condone that sort of reprehensible life style—it is antirevolutionary."

"What kind of car does the Party condone?"

"You're baiting me, but I've come to expect it. I drive a Morris Minor. I bought it used for sixty pounds several years ago . . . Now, I wish you would go. I have work to do." He sat down at his desk and carefully inspected the end of his pen for globs of ink-filled lint.

She thanked him and exited. In front of the house she noticed a scruffy old Morris. There was a copy of *The Philosophy of Ludwig Feuerbach* on the back seat, and not the condensed version, either.

She drove around aimlessly, thinking about the Lechwoods and the peculiarities of the case. Several blocks from Scott's flat, on Wigan Lane, she noticed a familiar auto parked along the kerb. It was definitely Baxter's rented red sedan. He was sitting in the front seat, pretending to read a newspaper, but it was already too dim to read. She parked in an inconspicuous position and watched him for an hour, but nothing happened. Darkness fell. Intrigued, but famished, she gave up and returned to the inn for dinner.

CHAPTER 7

"I CALLED THIS MEETING to brief everyone. I have the situation well in hand. Number one, I have spoken to the police and they share my viewpoint that under no circumstances must the details of this unfortunate incident get into the press," J.G. expostulated, chopping the air into orderly slices in front of his chest.

"Unfortunate incident! What is this, somebody fart in public?" Harry exclaimed. "We're talking about murder here, or hadn't you heard?" He shook his head in disgust and then cracked his knuckles one by one for emphasis.

"This is precisely the sort of remark that must be avoided. There is no murder without a corpse. We must remain optimistic. And I'll thank you not to interrupt, Harry! You have no respect for your elders," J.G. said severely.

"And neither do you, from the way I've heard you talk to your own father," Harry retorted.

"The boy's right," Beatrice chimed in. "You don't fool anybody but yourself." Bitter disapproval, her usual expression, showed in every line of her face.

Lettie looked at all the other faces in the room. They all looked strained. There was a miasma of dread . . . "Miasma of Dread," that would make an interesting title . . .

Miranda began to sob quietly.

"Sweet Christ, get a grip on yourself," J.G. said through his teeth. "This is no time for histrionics."

"Trust him to take over," Giles muttered testily, his back to J.G., as he helped himself to another gin.

"Kindly repeat that remark," J.G. challenged.

Lettie held her breath, uneasily awaiting a shocking scene; but Giles slunk away to a corner, defensively nursing his drink. Fortunately neither Owen nor Candy were present to add to the difficulties, Lettie thought gratefully.

J.G. launched into a pep talk about pulling towards a common goal, dauntlessly facing a mutual enemy, and about the sanctity of the family name. He was showing signs of going on all night, until Rollo threw his cigar into the fire and stomped out the door, bitterly remarking, "I might have known that you only called us here to listen to you spout a lot of bilge! Why I didn't retire in Borneo, I can't think!"

"Under no circumstances talk to the press," J.G. bellowed after him.

"We are all bright enough to figure that out without you telling us," Scott huffed peevishly. He sat close by his mother's side. She stopped sobbing and put a cigarette to her lips. He instantly produced a lighter and ignited it.

She patted his knee and said, "That's a luv, Scottie."

He said, "Of course, Mother. Go fix yourself up, you've ruined your makeup. And you've got a hair on your dress." He plucked it from her bosom. Staring at the hair, a look of acute consternation appeared on his face. He made an odd explosive sound and hastily threw it into the ashtray, then quickly made his way to the tea tray. As if to cover his embarrassment, he bit savagely into a bun and gulped some tea, which caused him to cough for several minutes.

"For God's sake, stop it, you'll drive us all waxy!" Harry complained. "Nobody can make such a production of coughing like you can."

"Leave your brother alone," Miranda commanded. "You know Scottie has always had a morbid fear of choking to death."

"But it's getting a bit lackluster by now. You'd think a boy genius like him could come up with some interesting new morbid fear to amuse himself with," was Harry's reply.

"If you're quite through squabbling among yourselves," J.G. intoned, resuming his posturing, "it is high time that you all listened to the voice of reason and learned to control yourselves. This damnable business is the inevitable consequence of behaving like the common ruck. I intend to personally discover who is responsible—"

"What Uncle is trying to say," Harry interjected, "is that

whoever murdered Grandfather must raise his hand this minute. Uncle has brought his riding crop along for the express purpose of dealing with the offender in the holy name of Lechwood."

"You go too far—" J.G. shouted, pulling Harry out of his chair by the front of his shirt. Harry took a swing that landed loudly on his uncle's jaw, causing him to fall back and release his hold.

"Harry! J.G.!" Miranda cried, pressing her body between them.

"Oh God, we're all going to kill each other," Beatrice wailed.

"Please, please, let's behave like Englishmen!" Lettie pleaded in placatory tones.

The dining room at the Boar exuded the requisite atmosphere for an elegant dining experience—candlelight, white linen gleaming snowy against dark wainscotting. Inspector Darian, drinking wine in solitude, was seated at a table facing the door. He rose and motioned to Julia. "Have you had dinner? Excellent, then we shall have it together."

"You're quite certain I'm not imposing?"

"Of course not! Whatever gave you that idea?" he exclaimed, pulling out a chair for her.

"You have a terribly preoccupied look." She sat down and quoted, " 'He looked as he does when he's writing verse or endeavoring not to swear or curse or wondering where he left his purse.' "

"You *are* a devil." He flashed her one of his devastating smiles. — *Oh my!*

The waiter came and they ordered trout and another bottle of Moselle. They chatted comfortably over the consommé, both avoiding any reference to the Lechwood imbroglio. By the time they were removing the spines from their trout, Julia had become aware of a soft incandescence hovering around his head. Was she seeing her first aura? She had had three— no, four—glasses of wine. His eyes seemed to shoot adoring

messages along beams of light—just like in Donne's poetry
. . . An odd, lilting piano piece by Satie was playing in her
head. She found him an astonishingly attractive man—with
almost as much superb charm and wit as herself. Nothing like
an appreciative audience to put sparkle into one's act.

Over coffee and trifle, Julia took a deep breath and, with
some effort, extricated herself from an amorphous, libidinous
cloud and asked (in what she hoped was a strictly business
voice), "Well, Inspector, what have you got on O'Reilly?"

Darian's relaxed countenance tightened slightly. A line appeared where his eyebrows met. His eyebrows reminded her
of moths; she couldn't fathom why. "Come now, let's not
spoil a delightful dinner."

"I'll trade information for information."

"Oh look, I'd managed to forget about the bloody mess,
thanks to the pleasure of your company. Let's not discuss it
now."

She propped her elbows heavily on the table, resting her
chin in her hand while watching him open his smart kidskin
tobacco pouch. He had an excellent manicure, his fingers
long, his hands broad. A signet ring on his right small finger
glowed warmly in the candlelight. She vaguely noted his
beautiful hands, then blinked and redirected her thoughts
towards the more immediate problem.

"My guess is that Beatrice's old Sparky died of arsenic
poisoning—hence your interest in the bottle on the potting-
shed shelf."

He reluctantly nodded, sucking his pipe to light it. The
tobacco caught with a crackle. He removed the stem from his
lips and said, "You're a remarkable woman."

Inspired by the praise, she boldly guessed, "You've found
the weapon that fired the bullet through the motorcycle tank.
It was one of O'Reilly's guns."

"My dear Miss Carlisle, you do confound me, in more ways
than one—" he began.

"I'm right, then." A triumphant smile lifted her lips.

"Yes. We found the weapon—down a well in Tadbleak."

She grasped the table and carefully leaned over to rummage through the enormous shoulder bag that lay at her feet. "Here we are." She produced a large brown paper sack and put it on the table. "Your reward for cooperating."

"What's this in aid of?" He doubtfully accepted the bag, peered inside, and removed one of the envelopes. "Soil samples from the potting-shed floor? Thanks awfully, but I've taken plenty of my own."

She indignantly thought, what kind of fool does he take me for? but said aloud in oleaginous tones, "Come now! Note the texture—obviously different from the stuff in the shed." Then she thought, what cheek I have! Why does a stuffed shirt like him put up with it? She wrinkled her nose and shrugged. "I beg your pardon, Inspector, I shouldn't try to teach Granny to suck eggs."

He laughed heartily. It was lovely—he could laugh for a living. Just then a quartet stepped up on the small stage across the room and opened with a dreamy number à la Brubeck. A few couples got up and shuffled around the dance floor.

"Dance with me."

"Oh gawd—it's so corny—"

"Not in the slightly quiffy condition we're in."

"Ah, well—"

"I insist." He rose and took her hand.

"I'd love to," she whispered in a breathless voice—a movie starlet swept gracefully into the arms of Lawrence Olivier.

She was grateful for the wine—otherwise it would have been too disturbing to suddenly be touching him—chest to chest, cheek to cheek. As he pulled her closer, she wondered what Margaret Mead would say about this titillating custom. They slowly floated to the bittersweet wailing of the saxophone. She inhaled the scent of aftershave and pipe tobacco, and felt very warm. The sax began to plead in silky, lascivious tones. Darian ran his lips softly across her ear.

The number ended. She reminded herself that custom dictated that when the music stops the couple must stop embracing and, pretending not to be aroused, make idle chitchat. Nothing but "your room or mine?" came to her mind. He obviously was having similar difficulties; but the waiter intervened to say that the inspector had an important call at the lobby desk. Darian nodded.

"Please excuse me," he said, like a man who had just mentally straightened his tie.

"Of course."

She studied his back as he walked away, and then unsteadily returned to her chair. The waiter returned with the inspector's apologies for having to take an abrupt leave of her charming company.

"He might have at least returned to say good night."

"He left in a great hurry, Miss."

Julia shrugged and carefully stood up. The waiter said good night and began clearing the coffee cups away. She thought there was something definitely melancholy about rumpled napkins and crumbs on plates. Someone ought to write a poem about it. Someone probably had.

Slightly under the weather, Julia was making her unsteady way to breakfast the next morning when Baxter came out of his room—just across the hall from her own. There seemed too much green corduroy trousers—nobody's legs could possibly be that long! He was wearing a white turtleneck sweater with a design of multicolored flying saucers across the front. In the morning light filtering feebly through the hall window, he looked very tanned.

"Are you from California?"

"Yes, Palo Alto. How could you tell?"

"Your tan—and your tailor."

"Do you like my sweater?"

"Oh yes. I admire a man with a penchant for whimsical clothes."

"A lady of discernment. Nice morning, isn't it?"

Yawning, she said that she hadn't looked yet.

"Neither have I, but I thought the English always wanted to discuss the weather—especially when meeting in hallways."

"What do Americans always want to discuss under similar circumstances?"

"I don't know. In fact, nobody seems to know what is expected of them anymore—a breakdown of rituals. Take holidays—the vitality has gone out of the myths behind those three-day weekends. So, feeling vaguely empty, the American hitches up his power boat, straps the dirt bike to the back of his Winnebago, and joins the lemmings on the freeways, in search of what he's lost."

"What's a win-a-bago?"

"A recreational vehicle."

"Oh. We call those caravans. Are we having breakfast together?"

"Sure. Talk about the magic going out of myths—I freaked when I saw Stonehenge—covered with spray-paint graffiti, and fenced in to keep the vandals out."

"Oh, I know! There's nothing like a can of spray paint to destroy eons of human history in fifty-two seconds."

"I'm also blown away by the juxtaposition of seventeenth-century gardens and gas stations. At home everything is new —so the tackiness of modern stuff isn't so apparent."

"Cheer up, you'll get used to it."

They found a table and ordered breakfast. While they waited, he took out his pocket calculator and explained the computer game he'd invented that morning. She squinted and politely tried to follow.

"Do you invent computer games for a living?"

"No. I'm an assistant research director for an electronics firm."

"Why did you come to see Sir Alfred?"

"I had to attend a symposium on software in London. This is a side trip. I've wanted to meet Sir Alfred for years. He's a demigod in the field. I'd love to get my hands on the craven bastard who murdered him . . ." He suddenly became a convincing picture of fury and frustration, as he scowled and crumbled a piece of toast in his fist. When she pointed out that he'd destroyed his toast, he seemed to quickly regain control of himself. "Oh well, what's one more piece of cold English toast? Why do they always bring it in a toast rack specially designed to give each slice maximum exposure to cooling air, so that it's always cold and hard when it reaches the table? And this," he held up another piece, "from a nation who uses egg and tea cozies."

"Oh, save us from this dastardly fate! Invent a toast cozy for us!"

"It would never sell. You all like your toast cold and hard —don't you?"

"I've never thought about it, actually."

"Because you've never had a hot piece of toast in your life," he declared, and abandoned the subject to inhale his breakfast. She had only just begun a doubtful preliminary poke at the yellow of her egg when he had devoured everything on his plate. He took a gulp of coffee and asked why the English called sausage "bangers." Julia said that she didn't know.

"Oh well, I've got to get my butt in gear," he said, putting on his sunglasses, justifying her impression that no Californian ever went outdoors with his naked eyeballs exposed. "Have a good one."

She wondered what he had been up to lurking in Wigans Lane, but doubted if he would answer if she asked him. He had an easy, friendly manner—but he also gave the impression of wary alertness.

"I think it would be a good idea if you beat me up later," she said.

His mouth dropped open comically, and then he said, "Beating up people isn't my idea of a high—not even an attractive lady like yourself."

"Whoops. There's a translation problem here—what did you think I was proposing?"

"Just that I blacken both your eyes—for openers."

She laughed. "Honestly, I was merely suggesting that you look me up later—that we get together."

"*That,* I can relate to—champagne, disco dancing, a moon-light drive on the Cotswolds, heads together, singing old Beatles tunes . . ."

"I was thinking more along the lines of a conference over a cup of tea."

"Who says the English don't know how to have a good time?"

Lettie and Julia met in front of the giant biscuit tin that housed Lechwood Electronics.

"Nothing on that girl . . ."

"What girl?" Julia asked.

"Harry's alibi. But there have been some interesting developments. I caught Miranda going through her father's desk —looking for the will, perhaps. And the police have got O'-Reilly!"

Sir Alfred's office was a small, unpretentious cubbyhole inhabited by his secretary, Mrs Cloves, a diminutive henna-curled woman with tiny black wing-shaped glasses that looked lonely on her broad pudding face. She seemed glad to see Lettie—they had mutual old friends in St Martin's.

When asked what it had been like to work for Sir Alfred for twenty years, she replied, with a tear in her eye, "Of course, I suppose he *was* eccentric, but after all these years I hardly noticed. He didn't act like a millionaire. He's been wearing the same dark wool trousers and leather flight jacket since I first came to work here. He was a proficient cyclist—fearless, you know. Occasionally he'd come in chuckling over a bad moment a patch of frost on the pavement had given him. But he only fell off twice in twenty years, which was a providence, since he didn't wear a helmet. I used to worry about him, but after a while, I came to think of him as immortal . . ." She gulped noisily and dabbed at her eyes. Julia felt a lump rising in her own throat. Mrs Cloves finally got her emotions under control by removing a file from the cabinet and thumbing through it, explaining, "I've been going through all the files. It's such a comfort knowing everything is filed properly; and one needs comfort in a situation like this."

"Don't worry, dear, it'll all turn out for the best," Lettie assured her in a kindly voice. "Do tell us more. You never know what might . . ."

"He was such a frail man—couldn't have weighed more than nine and a half stone. I was always amazed how little interest he took in money. In fact, he rarely carried more than a pound in his pocket. Several times he went off to lunch and had to come back to borrow money from me to pay for it."

The secretary observed that her boss had been nervous and upset recently. "He didn't ever confide in me, but I have eyes and ears! Everyone here could see that the relationship between Sir Alfred and J.G. had deteriorated. They'd been at odds over certain production matters. And Owen's presence seemed to aggravate the whole thing—he's a trouble-maker, that one."

"Owen's presence?"

"Yes he worked here for a couple of months. J.G. wanted him to learn the business. I gather the boy had never been interested until just recently. He was here awhile; then something happened between J.G. and his son. The boy hasn't been back. Sir Alfred had never been too keen on Owen being here. I heard him remark once that J.G. and Owen deserved each other."

"I understand J.G. had been pressuring Sir Alfred to retire."

Mrs Cloves nodded. "That caused bad blood between them. Personally, I'd noticed no evidence of diminishing mental capacities. He'd been perfecting some remarkable new device, which tends to indicate he was as keen as ever."

"A device!" Julia exclaimed with interest. "What device?"

The secretary didn't know because, as usual, her employer had been secretive about it. "But he said once that it could revolutionize the computer industry." She added that J.G.

knew of the device and had been pressuring his father to show him the schematics.

"It may be vital to know more about this. Is there anyone who might have information on it?" Julia asked eagerly.

"His lab assistant, Teddy Wineapple, would know more than anyone else. He did much of the supportive experimentation in the lab; but Sir Alfred never allowed him to be in on the actual development. Sir Alfred has a private lab next to Teddy's. It's locked and only Sir Alfred has the combination. It's constructed like a fortress—only one vaultlike door, solid brick walls with no windows. To my knowledge, Sir Alfred has never allowed anybody inside his lab."

"J.G. might resent that exclusion."

The secretary nodded emphatically. "It's been like the Cold War around here with the one faction on this side of the building and the opposing faction in J.G.'s office across the hall. He has a meek little Oriental secretary who works like the devil for him. She and I barely speak—it would have amounted to consorting with the enemy—an unpardonable offense."

Julia inquired if an American named Baxter had been in the office. Mrs Cloves hadn't met him. Julia then asked if she had ever heard of him, or seen a letter from him. The secretary answered in the negative.

"Could you go through your correspondence file—and phone bills—to double-check? He claims to be from Palo Alto, California." The secretary readily agreed to look.

The lab was down a long white corridor buzzing with neon. On the left was the large assembly room where a hundred workers, dressed like surgeons, sat at benches and wired little gadgets together. Beyond that room was J.G.'s office, and then the lab across the hall. A delicate-looking (à la Pre-Raphaelite) young man with silky shoulder-length blond hair and a reddish beard admitted them. He was clad in a white lab coat. They got a glimpse of tables of apparatus, an infinitude of dials and switches and screens, before he ushered them right back out. Teddy Wineapple politely refused to discuss anything at all, and disappeared back into his inner sanctum.

"Teddy is smart to keep mum," Julia remarked.

"Fortunately everyone isn't so smart, or we wouldn't . . ."

J.G.'s office was a spacious, elegant affair of marble and leather—quite a contrast to his father's. A young sturdy-looking Oriental woman smiled shyly at them from behind her typewriter. When they asked to speak to J.G. she said he was in conference. Julia chose to wait, but Lettie, mumbling something about an appointment, left.

The secretary, whose name was Yoko Okawa, made pleasant small talk of an outstandingly bland sort. They agreed that the weather was really quite warm for November. And Julia said what a pleasant area Tadbleak was—so much more relaxing than London. But Yoko said that London was such a wonderful city to live in, etc., etc. Julia learned in this roundabout way that Okawa had lived in London before, and had been at her present job for two years. And that she admired the Lechwood family immensely; and wasn't Callingwoods beautiful—even the name was lovely—and that echo! Weren't echoes just so fascinating, just like mirrors, really.

Julia had grown bored with these prosaic observations when several men emerged from J.G.'s inner office. Hands were wrung; arms were gripped; meaningless but encouraging-sounding phrases were exchanged; and all but one man left.

Julia rose as Yoko introduced her. J.G. ushered her into his office. He fixed her with a commanding stare and indicated a chair. She obediently sank into it, while he leaned against his black Italian marble-topped desk and folded his arms across his chest. "Frankly, Miss Carlisle, I consider your—as well as your aunt's—role in this affair superfluous, at best."

He wore a well-tailored grey suit of slightly luminescent material, white starched shirt, old-school tie. He had what would have been a fine, austere face, if it weren't for an aggressive chin usurping his nose's rightful role of leadership. His chin was made more obvious by a purple bruise. His eyes radiated almost as much warmth as a pit viper's. The family crest decorated his cufflinks, pen set, and cigarette lighter. Julia observed all this to amuse herself while he went on. "I entertain serious reservations re your ability to ameliorate the situation. I would have sent you both packing yesterday, but for the indication that your aunt's presence keeps Beatrice from doing something regrettable that might only add to the scandal. But be forewarned, if you aggravate me in any way, I won't hesitate to take action. Do I make myself clear?"

"Pellucidly so."

He signed heavily, and a look of magnificent sacrifice creased his brow. "I am doing my damnedest to keep the plant and the family together. The rampant degeneration of moral fibre in this country in the past twenty years is enough to make a strong man despair. But I am not despairing, Miss Carlisle. I shall weather this storm and emerge triumphant and unscathed."

"And hopefully with your father's latest invention safely in your fist," Julia couldn't resist remarking dryly.

His eyes narrowed. His nostrils flared as his powerful jaw muscles bulged like whipcord. "I don't know who is spreading this absurd rumour about a new invention, but let me put a stop to it here and now. My father has *not* recently perfected a new development—it was nothing more than a pathetic fantasy of a failing intellect. He couldn't admit to himself that he was fading, that he was no longer sharp enough to continue his lifelong work."

The phone rang; and she was perfunctorily dismissed.

She returned to Mrs Cloves' office to find her in conference with Lettie. "I've done the files. No record of calls or correspondence between Sir Alfred and Baxter."

"J.G. just flatly denied that Sir Alfred's invention existed."

Mrs Cloves looked disgusted. "I overheard them arguing about it only a few weeks ago. J.G. was very aware of the enormous monetary potential an important innovation could mean. He was, no doubt, already dreaming of the capital gains."

"But surely J.G. would get his chance to exploit the device once it was perfected."

Mrs Cloves had her doubts. She said no one could be certain what Sir Alfred's plans were; he had, after all, threatened to cut J.G. out of it altogether.

Julia considered this interesting possibility, then said, "But surely J.G. has quite a bit of power here. How could his father keep the device away from him?"

The secretary said the old man could buy another facility and maintain total control over the manufacture and sale of his device.

"I don't imagine J.G. would take kindly to something like that . . ." Lettie mused, imagining the outraged look on that supercilious face when he got wind of such a plan.

"In my opinion, J.G. would stop at nothing to prevent his father from excluding him from the project," Mrs Cloves gravely said, then made a reluctant little gesture, as if she feared she'd said too much.

To the secretary's knowledge, only a few people even knew of the device's existence—J.G., Teddy Wineapple, and herself. Sir Alfred was extremely secretive and so was J.G.—as industrial espionage was not an uncommon threat in the electronics field. Teddy Wineapple had come with impeccable references; but even after he had been at the lab for several years, Sir Alfred had never shown him the schematics of anything he was developing until it was ready for manufacturing. Sir Alfred personally supervised the installation of the alarm system himself and had told only her where the power switch was hidden.

"You mean, you could turn off the alarm system if you wanted?"

Mrs Cloves nodded.

"He must have trusted you more than anyone else in the . . . !" Lettie exclaimed.

The secretary nodded mistily. "It's a great honour—one I don't take lightly."

"If the alarm system is turned off, does it affect the impregnability of Sir Alfred's lab?" Julia asked. Mrs Cloves replied that the lab was so well constructed that it didn't require an alarm system. "I need to get into J.G.'s office at night. Would you be willing to help me?"

The secretary tapped her fingers on the top of her typewriter and looked extremely reluctant.

CHAPTER 8

". . . HAVE YOU HEARD ABOUT the scientist who found a way to combine the work of Freud and Einstein—and got sex at the speed of light?"

"Har! That's a good one!" Rollo guffawed so violently at this bit of sparkling telly wit that his cigar dropped from his mouth and, before he could retrieve it, singed away a green houndstooth on his plus fours.

Julia looked away in an agony of writhing sensibilities and turned her gaze to the photos on the mantel. There was a snap of Candy, voluptuous in a bikini, kneeling on a beach. A bit of trash could be seen blowing in the sand. There was a wedding picture posed in front of a mud wall—Candy straightfaced in an embroidered peasant dress, Rollo at least three inches shorter, cutting a squat figure in a white suit, a broad smile creasing the corners of his houndish eyes. The other photos were of a younger Rollo, dumpy in wrinkled bush get-ups, posturing over a variety of animals that looked —even in death—superior to the hunter. Even as a youth, Rollo wasn't much to look at. He had sad brown eyes, a pouchy face, with thick brows that curled up at the ends. He wasn't handsome enough, or ugly enough, to look interesting.

Julia shifted her gaze to Candy, who was curled up on the love seat sucking on a sweet and indifferently staring at the tube. Opening her pink-painted mouth, she revealed large, very white buckteeth biting a glistening red gumdrop. Heavy black eyeliner overemphasized her little, round eyes.

". . . Next we shall interview a Mrs. Jones from Boynton. She's an expert on carpet and really not bad on lino either." The blue, smirking face on the screen was slightly obscured by the thick, malodorous cigar smoke that fouled the air in the crowded little room.

"Ahargh!" Rollo waffled, grasping his sides in helpless mirth.

"What do you think happened to Sir Alfred?" Julia began.

Rollo, ignoring her question, leaned forward to catch the next joke.

Candy said, "A certain party got greedy and done Alf in before he could change his will."

"Who?"

"Oh, any of the lot might. We're one big happy family, aren't we? Hanging 'round waiting for the old fossil to croak. Only someone couldn't stick it another minute."

". . . I read in the papers about the perfect crime. Thieves broke into Scotland Yard and stole all the toilets. The police say they haven't a thing to go on."

"Ah ha ha!"

"Who couldn't wait another minute?"

Candy rolled her eyes and twirled a lock of bleached hair that made a halo of frizz to her shoulders. "None of us are is exactly rolling in dough, except for J.G., but money isn't enough for that one—he wants jam on it. Then there's Miles —a lush can have ambitions too," she snickered. "If only he had his wife's inheritance, he thinks he could make a fortune importing straw mats and prove to everybody he's a man after all. Except he'll never prove it to his wife."

". . . This year the national committee on sexual equality is holding its annual meeting at a nudist camp to air their differences."

"Air their differences! Har!"

Julia found herself wondering, along with the nephews, what magical attraction Rollo possessed for Candy. If it was money—there wasn't much in evidence, judging from the tatty furnishings and modest car out front. Of course, there was all that potential inheritance. She might have married for love, but what about her tawdry reputation? Vicious gossip?

Groundless rumour?

". . . And what would you tip the porter at a nudist camp? Will a pound note cover it?"

"Arrhh!"

"What do you think of the three grandsons? Are they desperate enough to murder for money?"

"You wouldn't think Owen would be desperate for cash, since J.G.'s got it in pots. But Daddy knows what's best and keeps it all for himself. As for Harry, he's got a mate on Wardour Street who needs a partner for his struggling film company—you know the sort, years ahead of their time and months behind in the rent. Harry would jump in in a flash, but he hasn't a shilling. Turning tricks for blue movies isn't the quick way to the lap of luxury." She offered Julia the candy dish. "Want a sweety?"

"No, thank you. And what about Harry's brother?"

"Scott says he isn't interested in money—only something called the revolution. It sounds like a lot of crap to me."

Julia was rapidly getting the impression that whatever she was, Candy was nobody's fool.

"So if inheritance is the motive—the whole family is suspect. But some have alibis," Julia remarked.

Candy uncrossed her legs and stretched her arms and arched her back, a gesture which made her pink shirt gap to reveal a bit of black lace. "I don't know who has one and who doesn't. All I know is that me and my husband were together all the time. I had a stomachache and Rollo nursed me."

"Did you have any visitors or phone calls between twenty past four and six?"

"No, but that doesn't prove we weren't here all along."

Julia stood up to go. Rollo looked up from the telly long enough to dismiss her with a wave. It was patently obvious that the telly wasn't the only reason for the snub.

Candy plucked a black gumdrop from the dish, popped it into her mouth, and said, "Don't mind showing yourself out, luv."

The fuel gauge was on empty—and here was a petrol station. Darian was in one of the several cars ahead of her at the pump. She tapped her horn. He looked around and saw her.

"I got the report on your soil samples this morning," he said as they leaned against her car for a chat.

"Any trace of arsenic and ground meat?" she asked. He nodded.

"Lovely."

"Well, don't just stand there looking smug. Where did you get the samples?"

"From the hole under the pheasant enclosure. I heard that O'Reilly had complained about Sparky digging under and killing the pheasants. Apparently it had happened several times before, so it seemed likely that O'Reilly might have taken it upon himself to eliminate the nuisance with a healthy dose of pesticide. Sparky ate the poisoned meat that evening, went into the house, drank the health drink and expired. This is all conjecture, of course, but substantiated by the soil analysis."

They gave their keys to an attendant and perched on a low wall at the side of the parking lot, where a boy in coveralls was waxing a gold Mercedes.

"You're a damned clever woman," he said. "And worth a lot of anyone's time."

"I do my best."

"You're blushing like a Victorian," he chuckled.

"It's rude to make that kind of remark to blushers, but never mind. Since I've caught you in a generous mood—tell me what news of Sir Alfred."

"No news yet."

"Isn't that odd?"

"A thorough local search can take weeks to unearth a body."

"And if it's secreted in a desolate spot a hundred miles from here?"

"Then it could be months—or never."

"But none of our suspects have had the time and opportunity to drive a hundred miles to dump the body—not without an accomplice. Aunt Lettie never uses an unknown accomplice in her books—says it widens the field too much and makes it an unmanageable problem to realistically solve in two hundred pages."

"Who says her books are realistic?"

"Not I . . . you know, the American bothers me. How do we know who or what he is?"

"We don't. I've cabled for substantiation, but it will take time to get it."

She nodded, absent-mindedly swinging her legs like a child sitting on a wall.

"You have beautiful legs."

She could think of no response. Her brain was becoming hopelessly muddled by the attraction between them. She wished he would tone down the intense stares, the ready smiles; it was bordering dangerously on puerile fantasy.

"To return to the subject, if I may, I'm disillusioned with the inheritance motive—doesn't fit the method. Industrial espionage as a motive seems so much more reasonable."

"It didn't take you long to twig to that one. Who told you?"

"Mrs Cloves—she's known Aunt Lettie for centuries."

He nodded. Julia stared at her feet. He said after a moment, "Have dinner with me again tonight. I promise this time I won't run out before the brandy."

"What *was* so urgent last night?"

"—Do you know, I almost just blurted it out!" He shook his head. "And me, the epitome of discretion. You're turning my head."

"Go on! It's been an equitable arrangement—"

He admitted that he had great hopes for the relationship. She avoided his eyes, concentrating on the little circles of wax on the Mercedes' fender. The boy smeared it on in slow, deliberate swirls. The sweet smell of wax reached her nose. She closed her eyes and breathed deeply. All this was going to her head—she had smelled car wax before, but had never felt the least bit . . . "Of course! Car wax!" she cried, jumping down from the wall and dancing elatedly. Darian obviously thought she had taken sudden leave of her senses. "Listen— I persuaded Scott's landlady to let me into his apartment. He came home smelling of car wax!"

"So?"

"So, I saw his car when I left—it obviously hadn't been waxed for months!"

"Forgive me, but it doesn't do a thing for me." He shrugged.

"All right. Maybe it doesn't mean a thing. He could have been helping a friend wax his car after work. Still—it might be a very significant detail."

"Please don't drop any more red herrings on my plate," he sighed.

"How does Scott's alibi hold up?"

"It's worthless, as a matter of fact." He revealed that the dentist, a Party member, had agreed to lie because Scott claimed he needed cover for a secret Party meeting. But the nurse, who knew Scott hadn't been a patient on November 10, was nervous about lying to the authorities. She had called the police station the previous night. When questioned again, the dentist admitted that Scott hadn't been there on the afternoon in question. The landlady's testimony that she'd seen Scott arrive home at six that evening could not be shaken.

On the quarry floor, Julia slowly marched around the circle of stones. "What a lovely place to perform pagan rituals!"

Lettie didn't share her enthusiasm. "I wouldn't know, dear, I never stoop to that disreputable pagan twaddle, although heaven knows it sells books."

Julia threw a stick for Tim, who dashed off after it, tail wagging furiously.

"You look radiant, dear. He is such an attractive . . . be careful not to fall in love with him—it's best not to get involved with the police . . ."

Julia dreamily examined the delicate red lichen growing on

a stone. "This quarry is loaded with phallic symbols, just like Miranda said."

"Julia, I can tell that you're not paying attention to my advice."

"What did you say?"

"I said do try to avoid losing your head over Inspector Darian."

Julia cheerfully assured her that she would take care, as she admired a line of naked willows, sinuously weaving in the wind.

"See that you do. It's disastrous to fall in love with a man who's engaged to be married—unless he's engaged to you, of course, then . . ."

"Crikey! He's engaged?! How do you know?" she gasped, her sheep's eyes suddenly opened.

"I pry. I ask questions that are none of my business; and because I'm a featherheaded old puss, I find things out."

"What else do you know about him?"

"I've seen him look appreciatively—most appreciatively—at women."

It was true, of course; that was how he looked at her, after all. Dashing a stone against the ground she asked what other women.

"That cute little Oriental secretary of J.G.'s."

"The randy clot! Bet he's heard that Oriental women are servile, just what his ego requires."

"Of course, we have no concrete evidence that he goes beyond looking—do we?"

Her niece replied that it would be evidence easily obtained. "If he's engaged, he has no right to act so damned interested!"

"You're right, of course, but that's precisely when some men become most interested in other women. Now, Julia, don't look so upset. Just be thankful you're not his poor affianced."

"Damn his eyes! Oh well, now I shan't feel so smarmy

ruthlessly picking his brain. He was most cooperative today."
She sighed and described her theory of Sparky's poisoning.
Lettie listened with growing elation.

"That's brilliant! So it had nothing to do with Sir Alfred,
after all! If only he had known! Having a paramedical background, when the dog died, he probably jumped to the con-
clusion that his recent leg and headache pains were evidence
of slow arsenic poisoning. No wonder the poor man . . .
Several people have substantiated that O'Reilly never locked
his door, by the way. Anyone could have helped himself to
one of his . . . And it's such a desolate spot, there's very little
risk of being . . . which reminds me, I overheard a nasty
go-round between the Poindexters today . . ."

She had been putting Tim's leash on in the hall when she
had heard loud voices from the second floor.

"Where the hell have you been? I know you haven't been
with that gardener scum—he's in the jug." Miles sounded
dangerously tight.

"I've had it up to here with you," was Miranda's heated
reply. "Either you get therapy, or pack up and get out of my
father's house!"

Julia considered the ramifications of the exchange, and
then shook her head in disgust. "Why some people stay married is a mystery to me."

Lettie said it was all most unfortunate.

When Julia related that Scott's alibi was broken and how he
smelled of car wax, Lettie considered it interesting enough to
warrant dedicating some time to keeping an eye on the boy.

"And what is your next step, dear?"

"I *had* planned to have dinner tonight with the irresistible
inspector—"

"Is that wise?"

"But I shall stand him up instead. Can you find out the
name of that London inquiry agent Sir Alfred hired? I think
I shall go look him up."

"Good idea."

"What do you think about this wonderful new industrial

espionage motive? I fancy it a lot better than inheritance. But, if it was very hush-hush, it would have to be someone with an inside source of information—and some contact in the industry to enable them to market it." She paused to consider the ramifications. "Or J.G. might have killed his father to prevent him from selling the device, or in some other way cutting J.G. out of the action. But J.G. has an alibi—of course, he *would*—but this silly wire business—I don't like it!" Just then Tim returned and insinuated himself into Julia's arms. "Oh! He smells like he's found the corpse!" She groaned, dropping the reeking animal. "Ugh—sorry for the ghastly quip."

Lettie kindly advised her not to be so glum; and Julia replied that she was doing her damnedest. "What about O'-Reilly? Surely he isn't moronic enough to fire his own rifle at Sir Alfred?"

"Don't you read the news? Often a murderer's lifelong friends are amazed when they hear what he's done. 'He was such a gentleman, such a nice, quiet chap,' they tell reporters. There are no limits to the heinous crimes one can read about. It's taught me one amazing thing about human nature . . ."

"Man's inhumanity to man?"

"No—well, yes, but that doesn't amaze me. It's taught me that some people just aren't squeamish."

"Like physicians."

London had a novel look, as if she'd been gone for ages, although it had been only days. She thought of her job with a mixture of guilt and relief strongly reminiscent of childhood truancy. Of course, she might not have a job by now. The thought conjured up a lovely vision of a new life style, living by one's wits, refusing to let mundanities like rent and utilities control one's destiny.

She found the inquiry agent easily. He lived in a shabby room above a Chinese laundry in a ramshackle section of Elephant and Castle. The smell of chemicals and fried garlic floated up the lopsided stairs. The Chinese shouting singsong at each other made it possible to close one's eyes and pretend to be in New York City, or Manila. The detective, middle-aged and unshaven, prodded at his molar with a letter opener and refused to cooperate. To quell the frustration, she told herself that here was a case who had lived by his wits too long. It had left him mean and surly.

Hands in pockets, she took in the trash-filled, shabby street. Her gloom had returned. She should probably ring up her employer at home and promise to be back at the desk the next day. Perhaps she should call up Siegfried and suggest a drink. But it would be dreary—he didn't have a sense of humour, at least not one that she could comprehend. *who ?*

She picked up the papers from the mat and wearily entered home. The familiar living room was at once comforting and depressing. She stretched out on the rug *?* and thumbed through the papers, noticing that the articles on the Lechwood case were sensational, but somewhat lacking in factual information. Her horoscope advised caution in dealings with goats and scorpions. The next page was adverts for flicks. Her eyes strayed to the pornos. *Naked as They Come, Brazen Equestrians, Podiatrists in High Heels, Video Sex Service.* The man's leg in the gritty little photo looked familiar. Her magnifying glass revealed that, yes, there was a distinctive heart-shaped mole on the left knee. That was Harry Poindexter's knee, all right! *Video Sex Service* was playing at the Starburst.

It was a small but motley crowd of winos and businessmen. There was only one other woman in the audience, who cornered Julia in the lady's lounge and confessed to being a female impersonator. He blotted his lipstick on a paper towel, licked a finger and ran it over his brows, while advising Julia where to get a simply sinful savings on wired pushup brassieres with cutaway cups.

The house lights dimmed. The curtains squeaked open. A bottle clanked to the floor and rolled down towards the front. The audience shifted in its seats. Someone had a nasty coughing fit. The cigarette smoke glowed blue against the screen.

The plot was a surprisingly ingenious takeoff on video dating services. Harry Poindexter, looking handsome in navy sports coat, white turtleneck, and red plaid trousers, was seated in one of the two molded plastic chairs in front of a plain blue screen. He made a few opening remarks explaining video dating services as they actually worked, then launched into a breezy social commentary to the effect that functioning in modern society had become so problematical that it was not surprising that so many people were willing to pay agencies to find them jobs, homes, and sexual partners. The advantage of video dating services over computer questionnaires was apparent: who could pick a hot number from some dull, computerized questionnaire that didn't even ask the right questions? But video dating service showed you tapes of interviews, enabling you to get a good long mouthwatery gape before you met the potential object of your lust.

The first interview began with Harry off camera firing questions at a plump redhead who sat on the edge of the chair next to him.

What did she do for a living? Had she ever had a quick one in a furniture store while the salesman was busy with another customer? Did she believe in reincarnation—if so, then didn't that make doing it with other species okay? What physical deformities did she like best? In the course of the interview, he sprang suddenly into view, grasped wildly at her gleaming plastic disco shoes, wrenched them roughly from her feet, and, grunting, nibbled on her toes.

Julia blinked in amazement at the speed with which he removed his clothes. Either they had tearaway seams, or the film was sped up slightly.

The next interviewee, a tall slim negress who taught Chinese, had a tattoo that said "smart ass." The third interview was with a bespectacled young woman claiming to be a graduate student of seventeenth-century poetry and Bergman films, but had obviously been most significantly influenced by the way Marilyn Monroe (or a tropical fish) had opened and closed her mouth. During a break in the action, the interviewer paused to trace a row of teeth marks on her left cheek and said in sudden Cockney "'Ullo, where'd you get that lovely refined scar?"

"A horse bit me."

"Go on!" he shouted. She clobbered him with a resounding wallop, and he roared à la Richard Burton, "Then crown my joys or cure my pain: give me more love or more disdain."

"Oh, you know Carew!" she cried. "He isn't read much these days."

At this point, Julia gasped, "Oh my gawd!"

The foreign-looking person in the polyester Edwardian jacket, who had been brazenly leering at her from two seats away, leaned over and casually asked, "Excuse me, are you free this evening?"

Julia glared at him and charged out the exit. He pounded down the alley after her. Convinced once again of the survival value of sensible shoes, she easily sprinted the two blocks to her Austin, her pursuer close behind. The engine sputtered to life as he clutched her door handle, tore open the door and grasped at her arm. Shrugging him off, she accelerated, then slammed on the brakes. He lost his grip on the handle and fell in a heap in the alley. She revved up the engine and tore away. In her mirror she saw him slowly dusting himself off.

CHAPTER 9

THE ALLEY BEHIND THE Lechwood Electronics plant was like a de Chirico painting. Odd shapes—rubbish bins, large wooden shipping crates, an oil drum—all had a sinister quality in the glow of the street light, which illuminated only one side of the alley. Wearing a trench coat with turned-up collar and a turned-down hat, a slim figure moved noiselessly through the shadows.

There was the slightest movement among the trash bins—a scraping sound—a rat or an alley cat. The figure paused, eyes searching the gloom, then continued a stealthy route along the edge of the building. A larger shape in the shadows moved and reached long arms out into the light. There was a muffled "Damn!" "Ow!" A scuffle ensued—but a very quiet one—until the larger figure succeeded in pinning the smaller one against the wall.

"Oh, it's you. Hey—I'm sorry. Are you okay?" Baxter whispered, retrieving her hat.

"Nothing serious, just a heart attack. What the hell are you doing here?" Julia demanded, noticing how he obscured most of his face with the collar of his sweater.

"I thought I'd try my hand at breaking in."

"Why?"

"Same reason as you—to get the facts, ma'am."

"But how did you expect to get by the alarm system?"

"I know a thing or two about alarm systems."

"Is that right? Are you a professional international thief?" He laughed. "Well, never mind, I arranged to have J.G.'s office window open and the alarm system turned off."

"Terrific. We might as well go in together."

Julia hesitated, and then decided to adopt a wait-and-see attitude. As they skulked along the building towards J.G.'s window, she entertained serious doubts about breaking and entering with this person she knew nothing about. What if he were the murderer? Perhaps he was using her to steal the device, which would make her an accomplice.

The sash moved with a gentle push. The loyal Mrs Cloves had not failed her. If all went as it should, they would have an hour before the janitor arrived.

"Don't turn on any light or make a sound until I say it's okay. Be prepared to bail out and split if I give the signal," Baxter said, giving her a leg up and in. He then carefully heaved himself in after her. She waited just inside the window, listening to him moving surreptitiously along the walls. It seemed like an eternity before she heard him return with his torch lit.

"What was that in aid of?"

"I was checking for hidden video cameras," was his soft reply.

"Mrs Cloves said nothing about that."

"Maybe she didn't know about it."

"Well, did you find any, for God's sake?"

"I took care of it."

"What kind of an answer is that?"

"Are we going to stand here bickering all night, or are we going to case the joint?"

"Oh, all right." She turned on her torch and began methodically going through J.G.'s desk. She'd been at it awhile when she suddenly looked up and noticed that Baxter was no longer in the room with her. She pushed the drawer closed with a sinking feeling that he was pocketing the device while she was shuffling like a fool through J.G.'s papers.

He wasn't in the hall. Wondering if it would be best to prowl the rest of the plant, she thought she heard a motor pull up and stop outside. She tiptoed across the office and listened at the window, heart pounding in throat. To stay or to go? If it was the police, she'd be better off outside than in. But where had Baxter gotten to? Perhaps he'd gone out another way. But why would he leave without telling her? Was this some sort of impromptu frame-up? As soon as that possibility dawned, she immediately evacuated the building, pulled the window down, and then crept back towards the alley. She turned the corner. A film clip of a star going nova flashed in her eyes, as she plummeted into deep, dark space.

The street was moving beneath her, but not in the usual manner. She was looking down at the street from a viewpoint that was definitely peculiar. Was this walking on one's hands? If it was, it was giving her a horrible headache. No, her hands were just dangling there, not reaching the ground at all. There was something wrong with this, but it was too deep a subject to go into just now.

Then she was being folded into a car. She was afraid. She tried to scream, but a hand pressed so tightly against her mouth that it hurt her lip. She bit a finger. He swore and vigorously shook his hand. "Cool it, Tiger, it's only me, your partner in crime." Baxter's face appeared close to hers. He looked angry, even dangerous.

"You bastard, why did you hit me?" she groaned, as she turned her head and fireworks splashed across her line of vision. An alarm rang in her ears.

"I didn't."

"Where are you taking me?"

"To the hospital, obviously. I found you knocked cold in the alley. I could hear your brains rattling around as I carried you."

"What?"

"You might have a concussion. You ought to have your head examined."

"How do I know *you* didn't hit me?"

"I'm taking you to the hospital, aren't I?"

"I don't know."

"Don't get paranoid. Can't you feel that we share the same karma—decency, niceness, and all that right-on crapola?"

"You're an odd bird," she told him, wincing in pain as she moved her head to look at his dim profile. "I don't know what to make of you."

"Don't worry, it's a linguistic problem. It would be a lot of work, but we could clear it up in a few months, you know; intense daily rap sessions, some heavy toe tuggings, followed by aura massage, and maybe even a little—"

"Don't make me laugh." The electric wire zinging had begun oscillating in frequency.

"Did you see or hear anything before they punched your lights out?"

"Nothing. It could have been you."

"Shut up. You're starting to bore me." He tapped the steering wheel with his long fingers, whistling a lively tune through the split in his teeth.

The next thing she knew, she was leaning against him, his long arm firmly around her shoulders. Her rubber legs kept inventing new steps. The light was too bright. The doctor glared into each eye and fussed around a bit. He then diagnosed that she wasn't concussed and advised Baxter to put her immediately to bed. She slept through the drive back to the inn and the walk to her room.

The moment she woke, she knew it was late—but the clock had stopped. She must have forgotten to wind it the night before. The night before! A ginger touch to the bump on her head set waves of pain thudding dully through her skull.

After a long soak in the tub which improved the outlook somewhat, she slowly dressed and made her painstaking way downstairs, careful not to make any sudden moves.

There were only two people in the lobby—a middle-aged woman reading a magazine and an oldster carving a piece of wood. The clock on the reception desk read half past two. Could it really be that late?

Her stomach rebelled at the scent of hot grease as she passed the dining room and went out the side door to the parking lot. She squinted and blinked and gaped until she was finally convinced that the Austin wasn't there. Someone had stolen her car! Indignation made her head throb more violently until she realised that Baxter had driven her back. Her

Austin must still be where she had left it the previous night. Oh, well, a walk might clear out some cobwebs.

The tree-lined old section of Tadbleak abruptly became the barren new section of tract homes, which then merged into the industrial area. She ambled down Wigan Lane, where Baxter had been lurking two evenings previously, and made a mental note to come back tonight and see if he was there.

Her car was parked in the same spot—a few blocks behind the plant. The alley where she'd been coshed revealed no dropped matchbook, no button, nothing but the usual litter —candy wrappers and newspapers. She sat on a packing crate and thought about Baxter. He was up to something, to be sure. It was difficult to shake the impression that he was the one who had hit her. Why was she so certain? Had she subliminally noticed something that the blow had temporarily made her forget?

"Ah, lass, I can tell by your face you've got a crow to pick with me," Harry drawled between pants. The rope made that familiar snicking sound every time it touched pavement, reminding Julia of snatches of gruesome jumping rhymes—"I had a little brother, his name was Tiny Tim, I put him in the bathtub to teach him how to swim . . ."

"I was in London yesterday and caught *Video Sex Service.*"

"And what is your judgement—terribly refeened, what?"

"I don't feel qualified to comment."

"Come on, because you're not a film critic?"

"No, because I'm not a gynaecologist."

"Ha ha ha." He dropped the rope and zipped up the jacket of his sweatsuit. White mist steamed off his back and shoulders. His face was scarlet. "You don't approve of me, do you? Actually, I only have the morals of a proverbial tom cat on film —that's not as reprehensible as pranging that many in reality."

"You're saying that doing it in front of the camera isn't doing it in reality?"

"Right. We're all actors. Everyone's aware that it's a script. Nobody gets hurt."

"But you're still actually *doing* it, aren't you? Oh, never mind. My head isn't clear enough for conundrums today."

"If you haven't come to discuss sex and reality—its use and abuse—you must have come to talk about my alibi."

"Don't look now, but you haven't got an alibi. The maid overheard your film sound track."

"But I never intended it to be an alibi. I was innocently alone in my room listening to the sound track."

"Why?"

"To study my vocal versatility—is my brogue accurate, that sort of stuff. I never expected someone to overhear it and mistake it for reality—I beg your pardon, reality again. Anyway, you could have knocked me over with a feather when that pompous inspector—"

"He is a bit pompous, isn't he?"

"Starchy, condescending charlie, I say. Anyway, my mind was boggled when he took me aside and ordered me to reveal my alibi's name. I said that there had been no lady in my room. Then I twigged to what had happened. And I thought —what the hell—an alibi might come in handy in these troubled times, even if it did blot my copybook."

"Why should I believe you?"

"Use your head, girl. If I were going to set up a realistic-sounding film for an alibi, it wouldn't be that one. Interviews with a half dozen different women? Who would believe it— my room isn't big enough. Come on upstairs, I'll show you my tape recorder—and my etchings, if you like. But you've seen them already, haven't you?"

She remained just inside the doorway as he pointed out that the tape machine was in plain sight on a shelf beside his unmade bed. There was a clutter of tapes and underwear, a few crumpled beer cans on the floor, along with a copy of a sports weekly. "You see? I'm not even trying to hide the evidence. The cops looked right at it when they went through my room. Oh, come on, you look like a silly ass hovering in the doorway. Afraid to get too near the bed?"

"No, afraid of being mugged."

"Hah! Me, the sinister type? Not bloody likely."

"You are good at putting on an act—"

"Thank you. But all the world isn't a stage. I'm being straight with you, that should be as plain as the nose on your face."

"I can't trust anyone at this point."

He flung his arms up in a gesture of impatience.

"Have you been to bed with Candy Lechwood?"

"Who hasn't? They don't call her the village bicycle for nothing."

"What a hypocritical, chauvinistic remark—especially coming from you!"

"Don't get your knickers in a twist."

"Who else has she done it with—facts, not rumours, please."

He stretched out on the bed, his hands behind his head, his face screwed up in an exaggerated expression of concentration. "I know for a fact that J.G. walked in on her and Owen once. They were stoned and fooling around in the garage. J.G. threatened to kill her. In return, she threatened to blackmail him."

"When was this?"

"Sometime in September. Owen had started going in to learn the business like Daddy's good boy. Then Candy took a sudden interest in him. I'd gotten the impression that she'd rejected the boy's impassioned pleas before that. I think she purposely picked up on Owen to flaunt J.G. The girl's got guts—or else she's a very dim dumpling."

"She doesn't strike me as dim."

"Anyway, the next day Owen was out on his ass. J.G. ordered him out of his factory and out of his house. Jane had to produce some sort of fit to keep her only baby in the house. Makes you want to puke, doesn't it?"

"Does Rollo know about this?"

Harry shrugged. "I don't know. I wouldn't put it above J.G. to confront him with it. But if he knows, Rollo hasn't revealed it to the rest of us."

"Poor Rollo."

"Yeah. Poor bugger—not such a bad egg—just one fatal flaw; but according to the Greeks, that's all it takes . . . Then there's Teddy Wineapple, Candy's having it off with him."

"Your grandfather's lab assistant? The plot thickens!"

"Doesn't it just? I play squash in Tadbleak late Wednesday afternoons, then run back. I take the village road to the Beeches road, then across the park to here. There's a private spot overgrown with bushes just off the road to the Beeches. Once I ran by, and saw a spot of blue among the foliage. I investigated—it was Teddy Wineapple's Dolomite. The windows were all steamed up."

"Circumstantial evidence."

"I have a dirty mind. The car was rocking, but they were probably just innocently practicing their disco dance routine. His Dolomite's been parked there every Wednesday for at least a month."

"Are you certain it was Candy?"

"I heard her voice—I'd recognise that whine anywhere."

"It could have been a tape recording."

"Cheeky bitch."

CHAPTER 10

BEATRICE SAT ALONE in the huge living room. Her tear-stained eyes stared at the blue dog-show ribbon she fingered in her lap.

"He went insane, that's the only explanation for what he did to Sparky. There are strains of instability in this family, a queer quirk of the blood. I've been having nightmares about it—my own brother—who will be next?" she asked in dramatically stentorian tones, raising her haunted eyes to Julia's.

"It's not as bad as all that," Julia assured her, and asked if she'd seen Lettie. Beatrice hadn't, not since the previous afternoon. Julia rang for the butler, asked him to find Lettie, and whispered that someone should be keeping an eye on Beatrice.

The butler cast a discreetly nervous glance at Beatrice and hurried away. The maid came in with tea. Julia asked her if Lettie had spent the previous night at Callingwoods. The maid said Lettie hadn't slept in her rollaway bed in Beatrice's room. Julia called the inn. Lettie hadn't taken a room there. There were no other hotels in town.

Upstairs in the Poindexters' flat, Miranda, splendid in a long purple smock and matching scarf dotted with batik cabbages, was finishing up an elongated nude of her son, Harry. She had made his feet extremely large. She had caught him in the process of donning his athletic supporter.

"Hullo. They've let O'Reilly free today! Does this mean they no longer suspect him?"

"I don't know."

"Tell me everything you've found out. You were over at the plant, I understand."

"Who told you that?"

"My brother, of course. He was probably rude to you." She grimaced, dipping her brushes into a jar of turpentine. "J.G. has never learned any sympathy for anyone. He's got the sensitivity of a mollusk. My father's obsession with the efficiency of machines—it produced J.G."

"Have you seen Lettie lately?"

Miranda wiped her brushes on a rag and said she hadn't seen Lettie since yesterday, and then resumed her analysis of her brother. "We were all shocked when J.G. married. He'd never been interested in women. I was convinced that he was totally asexual. Of course, Jane obediently became an invalid—don't tell me *that* isn't some indication of their sexual problems."

Taking one more look at Harry with swollen pedal extremities, Julia asked the artist if she planned to hang it in her bedroom. (what's the point here?)

Miles was coming up as Julia was going down. His eyes were extremely bloodshot. He had the dogged air of a man barely surviving a perpetual hangover. He said he hadn't seen Lettie for days and didn't give a damn.

"Where's the phone?" she asked the butler, who met her in the hall with a report that Lettie wasn't anywhere to be found in the house. "I have some calls to make."

Same place it was on the last page I would imagine. . . .

The pub was filling up. A noisy dart game was in progress, a rerun of a football game on the telly. The chanting of the crowd and the nasal enthusiasm of the announcer on the box mingled with the conversation in the room. Darian sat at the bar over a pint. For a moment Julia stood and watched him conversing with the landlord, before she was able to approach him with a semblance of calm. His face lit up when he saw her.

"It was a lonely dinner last night," he said. "I was worried and a little annoyed."

"Something came up." Her voice sounded apologetic, in spite of herself. An authority-figure sex appeal, that's what it was, she thought.

"What's the matter?"

"I need your help."

"It's yours." They stepped out into the foggy night air,

108

buttoned up their coats, and walked along the green. "What is it?"

"Lettie—I can't find her. She didn't sleep at Callingwoods last night. She didn't sleep here at the inn. No one has seen her since yesterday." Anxiety was strident in her voice. He frowned and cursed. She sighed dejectedly, "I know this is the sort of thing you warned me about. I hated to have to come to you—but I've called everyone and looked everywhere I could think of."

"What do you mean, you hated to come to me? You should have come to me at once," he snapped, abruptly turning on his heel. She followed him back into the lobby. He called the police station, and then motioned to two of his men in the bar.

"What year is her estate wagon?"

"A 'fifty-two, I think. I don't know the number."

Darian quickly instructed his men. Julia bit her lip and listened with half an ear as she considered Lettie's announced intention to concentrate on Scott. Julia had knocked him up at his flat an hour before. He had reluctantly let her in, claiming he hadn't seen Lettie in days. Julia had rudely pushed past him and peered into all three rooms, but saw no likely place to stash a little old lady. There wasn't even a closet—just a rail with a few clothes hanging on it. Scott had indignantly ordered her out.

The police went off and Darian, exuding a paternal air of concern, turned to her. She longed to throw herself sobbing against his chest. He opened his arms, as if reading her mind. She backed away, mentally battening down the hatches. She wouldn't break down in front of him. "Don't back away from me," he quietly said.

She dumbly shook her head and strode out to the parking lot. He ran after her, calling, "Where the devil are you going?"

She told him Lettie had planned to follow Scott. "He's my only lead. I'm going to stake out his place."

"We'll take my car. It has radio contact."

In awkward silence they sat on the street below Scott's flat, beneath street lamps that glowed dimly in the fog. He finally said, "You're understandably worried and distraught—but why so withdrawn? I wouldn't have expected you to respond this way in a crisis."

"What do you know about me? Or I about you?" Her reply was tinged with some asperity as she thought, I know that you're engaged, that's what I know, although you don't know that I know.

"That sounded like some sort of indictment."

"I don't want to discuss it. If I sit in this car with you all night, I shall go mad! I can't stick it a minute longer!"

"In that case, let's confront him," he said evenly. "Perhaps I can intimidate him. But my legal role is delicate. I can't actually accuse him of anything."

"I can. I'll bluff him. You back me up by looking sternly menacing—you're awfully good at that." His growing irritation was obvious, but he made no comment. "Let's go, then."

He leaned forward and peered up at Scott's building. "Wait."

Someone appeared on the porch. It was Scott.

From a discreet distance, they followed his modest little Morris through the streets of Tadbleak. He took a narrow road towards Chumley's Wattle, a village five miles south. The thickening fog made it difficult to keep his taillights in view. Several times they thought they'd lost him, but eventually caught sight of him again. He finally pulled into a dirt lane and disappeared. Darian parked and said, "We'll go in on foot —the element of surprise is <u>abecedarian</u>, my dear Watson."

"Please don't bother trying to jolly me along."

They picked their way up a lane that sloped steeply for a half mile of a tree-studded rise to a magnificent little stone house with a large garage. The Morris was not in evidence.

"Shall we break in or politely ring the bell?"

"We reconnoiter," was his reply.

There were only a few illuminated windows at ground level. One was the kitchen, where Scott laboured over a gleaming copper-topped stove, while stuffing a huge slice of chocolate cake into his mouth. No one else could be seen.

They circled the house, noting the light in a second-story window above the porch.

"We could shimmy up the porch support and take a peek," she whispered.

"Might make too much noise if we both go up. I'll climb. You stay here."

"I'll go. I'm lighter—I'll be quieter."

"Then be careful for God's sake!"

She nodded and leapt lightly up onto the railing. Wrapping her limbs around the post, she slowly hauled herself up with arms and knees. She grasped the edge of the porch roof and, with some difficulty, heaved her weight up sideways. The roof was slanted, which made it necessary to crawl along it, crab-like. She clung to the windowsill and raised her chin up to the pane.

It was an elegantly appointed room in lavenders and blues, with a rose-coloured marble fireplace and a sinuous Art Nouveau bedstead inset with stained-glass lilies and iris. A brown velvet Morris chair sat in front of the fire, facing away from the window. A ball of pink yarn was twitching slightly on the rug beside the chair. Tim was snoring beside the fire. Julia could see an elegant silk bedsheet tied in a huge knot across the back of the chair.

She tried the window, but it was locked. She gingerly eased herself down the porch roof, clutching at the thick cedar shingles to keep from sliding off. She felt one of her fingernails rip, and caught a wool trouser leg on a nail.

It was easier to get off the roof than it had been to scramble up. She swung down, slid down the pole, and landed lightly on her feet beside the inspector.

"Graceful as a monkey!" he said softly. "I can see by your face that she's all right."

"Yes, I think so. She's up there. Tied to a chair with a sheet."

He put his arm around her shoulder and impetuously

hugged her. "Come along, then, we'll get her out of there."

For a moment Julia felt her armour dissolving. Other women had married lovers, after all. But if they were madly in love, how could they possibly compromise? How could they tolerate the hours he spent with his wife? She shrugged out of his grasp and climbed the front steps. The door was unlocked. They entered quickly. Darian went to find the kitchen; Julia ran straight up the stairs towards the light.

"Julia!" Lettie exclaimed joyously, dropping a stitch in her excitement. "Thank heavens! I was so worried about you!" Tim opened an eye.

"Worried about *me?*"

"I knew you'd be frantic when you missed me."

Blinking back tears, Julia stooped behind the chair and tugged at the knotted sheet. "He didn't hurt you, did he?"

"Oh, no, dear! Scott's really a very gentle young man who wouldn't harm a . . ."

"I wouldn't call kidnapping exactly harmless."

"He promised he'd set me free in two more days. Just as soon as his big deal went through. Something to do with stocks and futures. He explained it, but I didn't follow a . . ."

"That's got it," Julia gave a last tug and the knot loosened. Lettie stood up and smoothed her dress.

"He even bought me some very expensive pink wool and a most challenging bedjacket pattern."

Julia hugged her fiercely. "If you keep disappearing, my hair shall soon be as grey as yours."

They went arm in arm down the stairs. Darian, with Scott in tow, was waiting for them. Gnawing at his fingernails and sweating profusely, Scott silently stared at the floor.

"Now, now, Scott, don't worry, everything will be fine." Lettie patted him on the arm. He gave her a plaintive look, but seemed incapable of speech.

"I trust you are unharmed, Miss Winterbottom?" Darian inquired.

"Perfectly, thank you."

"I'm very glad. Mr Lechwood is accompanying me to the station. Here are the keys to his Morris. It's in the garage," he told Julia. "Take your aunt to the inn and put her to bed." Julia nodded. He led Scott off down the driveway to his sedan.

"Look at this!" Julia gasped as they entered the garage. Parked next to the little Morris was a posh new Daimler, waxed and gleaming. "Ah, the sweet smell of car wax!"

"It looks very expensive!"

"Twenty thousand pounds worth."

"No wonder the poor boy was on thorny ground—he *has* been overextending himself!" Lettie tsked.

As soon as Lettie was tucked in, Julia went down to the bar, too keyed-up with leftover jitters and curiosity about Scott to sleep. She ordered a pint and wondered when Darian would get back. He was staying in Room 10—just two rooms away from hers. She had another beer and thought what an acrimonious bitch she'd been to him that night. If only he had been honest with her and said, "Look, I'm engaged, but I'm wild about you." No, that still wouldn't have been any good; but at least she could have respected him for being forthright. As it was, he was just leading her down the garden path, the cad.

There was a soft tap at her door. She groggily opened one eye. The travel clock said two. She stumbled across the room, momentarily unable to recognise the surroundings. A man was standing in the dim light of the hall, his face obscured in shadow. She cringed and opened her mouth to scream. He pulled her towards him and held her cheek against the front of his cold trench coat. "Wake up, Julia, it's me." She recognised the vaguely herbal scent of Darian's aftershave. "I got your note."

Now wide awake, she disentangled herself and turned on the light. "What ungodly hours you keep!" She rubbed her eyes. "I thought I would stay awake and wait for you; but I must have nodded off."

"I was reluctant to wake you—but your note said it was

urgent that we talk tonight. Be that as it may, I'm now glad I woke you—you look like an adorable little girl with pink cheeks and rumpled hair." He touched her hair. She quickly retreated, straightening her clothes, and stepped into her shoes.

"I need some fresh air to clear my head. Can we take a short drive and talk?"

"Of course."

"You do look shagged. Do you mind?"

"I am tired; but I don't mind."

"I'll drive," she said. He helped her slip into her coat.

"Dress warmly, the weather has taken a turn."

She wrapped a bright yellow woollen muffler around her neck and they went out into the night. Feeling detached and disoriented, Julia drove slowly through the streets. The fog had thickened to pea soup stage.

"Why did Scott kidnap my aunt? And what's the story on those posh digs and motor?"

Darian explained that Scott, obviously aware that he could be charged with kidnapping, had insisted that he would have released Lettie unharmed in two days. She had apparently followed him to his house at Chumley's Wattle. She had seen his shiny new auto, and had refused to believe his story that he was house-sitting for a wealthy friend. His monogram, after all, decorated the gold screen in front of the fireplace and the silk shirts in the closet. Desperate, because he knew she couldn't be trusted to keep mum, he felt that there was no choice but to hold her prisoner until his big deal went through. The purchase of the extravagant car had been foolish. If the deal collapsed, he would be in dire straits.

"A double life! It does have a certain hypocritical charm."

"He claims it didn't start that way." Being something of a genius, Scott had studied the effect of labour strikes and other aspects of political pressure on the behaviour of stocks and securities. He was in a rare position—privy to inside information about when the Socialist Party would make their power plays. There came a time when he could no longer resist surreptitiously putting his theories into action. He began by investing his meagre savings. Eventually he had acquired quite a bit of capital—but had to keep it secret from his employers, the Socialist Party, and from his fellow comrades. They would have considered his activities unethical, not to mention antirevolutionary. It became a fascinating form of gambling, sucking him in. He even decided to sample a classic bourgeoise life style as well. "The double life aspect gave him great pleasure. Then he saw a chance to almost double his fortune—it was a complicated, fairly risky deal. He had all his capital tied up—and at that crucial point, Lettie walked in on him."

"Auntie said he was very decent to her. He kept her tied to the chair, but came three times today to cook and let her walk around. She believes he really would have set her free."

"He swore this deal was to be his last. If he won, he'd quit the Party and his job, move permanently into his house, and write a book on economics. If he lost, he would lose everything to his creditors. He would have to remain at his job and never gamble again."

"But why was it so important to take such drastic measures to keep Auntie quiet?"

"If the Socialist Party got wind of what he was up to, they could have queered the deal somehow—by not making a move that he was counting on them to make."

"What are you going to do with him?"

"It's up to your aunt to press charges."

She had taken the route to Callingwoods, but the fog was so thick in this area around the river that she had slowed to a crawl, unable to make out the pavement four feet in front of her headlamps.

"These are filthy conditions."

"Yes, better stop," she agreed, pulling over to what might have been the verge, and turned the key. He switched on the map light, which illuminated their faces from below in an amber glow with dramatic black shadows.

"Scott claims he was in London executing his deal on the

afternoon of the motorcycle incident. We'll verify that, of course."

They sat in silence for some moments before she commented that she'd lost her bearings. He said he thought they'd gone just past O'Reilly's cottage, about three miles beyond the long bridge.

She told him about Candy and Wineapple, and Candy and Owen, concluding, "which means we can surmise that Candy and Owen might know about Sir Alfred's invention. I think Baxter might know too."

"It's obvious how Candy might know—from Wineapple or Owen. But how would Baxter know?"

She rubbed the tender bump on her head, knowing it would be unwise to tell him about breaking into the plant with the American. She suspected that Baxter might be after the device, but had no clearcut, non-self-incriminating evidence. "Sorry, I can't divulge my source of suspicion at this time, but," she added, interrupting his indignant noises, "I discovered something interesting in London last evening."

"What were you doing in London instead of having dinner with me?"

"I went to see *Video Sex Service.*"

"Thought that might be more stimulating than my company, did you?"

"I suppose you couldn't resist saying that, so never mind. The film includes the following scene . . ." She repeated the dialogue verbatim.

"Good God!"

"Precisely what I said. The charlie next to me misinterpreted my excitement and made a grab in the alley—"

"You little fool! To take such asinine risks!"

"—So I had to rough him up a little. Then I came back here and confronted Harry with his phony alibi."

"Wha—" he sputtered.

"He seemed to have a plausible explanation . . ." While she repeated what Harry had said, Darian took out his pipe and puffed furiously.

"That was extremely precipitate!" he said irritably, shaking his head. "You should have told me about this. I never would have let you take the matter into your own hands."

"You're right, of course. I got carried away and before I knew it, I was tossing it in his teeth." The strong, sweet smell of the pipe made her slightly dizzy. She opened the window.

"He might have murdered you, as Scott might have murdered your aunt. I want you out of this business, dammit. You're both going home tomorrow."

She only said, "Let's go back and get some sleep."

He sighed heavily. "Shall I drive?"

"No, I can manage." She reached for the key, but he caught her hand.

"Julia, look at me." He took her chin in his other hand and stroked her cheek. "I know this has probably been very obvious to you . . ." He traced her lips with his finger. "I want to make love to you."

For a moment she was completely at a loss. Then she heard her voice saying, "Have you made reservations for the potting shed? It's booked so far in advance—"

The expression on his face silenced her. He took his hands away.

"That was a particularly nasty remark. But you've made your point." His voice shook with anger. He closed his eyes and looked away.

"I'm sorry. That was cruel. But I happen to know that you're engaged. Were you planning to tell me that before or afterwards?" When he didn't answer, she added after a moment, "I know lots of people do it, but that doesn't make deceit any less shabby."

"What kind of heartless bastard do you take me for?" he snapped.

"I don't know you well enough to answer that."

Starting the motor put an end to the tense silence. She turned the car around and crept along for what seemed like an eternity before the entrance pillars of Callingwoods appeared on their right, and faded back into the murk. She stole a look at him. He was leaning against the door, his hand over his eyes. There was some comfort in the thought that he might be feeling as wretched as she did. Perhaps she ought to follow his orders and leave tomorrow, just to avoid seeing him again. He probably could solve the case well enough without her. Then he could go back to London to his fiancée.

She saw the headlamps a moment before she heard the horn. For a terrible second, she thought the car was coming right towards them. Gritting her teeth, she braked and swerved.

"Stop the car!"

"I am," her voice quavered. She breathed a sigh, realising that the headlamps were stationary.

He grabbed the torch from the glove compartment and they dashed towards the lights. The blaring horn seemed loud, yet muffled by the weather.

"That's J.G.'s Mercedes."

It had gone off the wrong side of the road and smashed head-on into a tree. The windscreen was cracked like a spider-web—where the driver's head had hurtled into it. The tree was torn in half.

They tugged at the crumpled doors, but couldn't open them. Darian trained the torch on a bloody, broken figure pinned behind the steering wheel, which had been thrust several feet into the passenger compartment. Julia took one look at the remains of Owen Lechwood and turned away, struggling with an impulse to vomit.

"Sick?"

"No. Where are you going?"

"I've got to take a quick look around before we go for help." They followed the skid marks, which indicated the victim had crossed the river from the direction of Tadbleak. They had covered several yards from the smashup when Darian grunted and knelt down on the verge. Julia knelt beside him.

There were four round imprints about an inch deep in the gravel, forming a rectangle with nine-inch-by-eighteen-inch dimensions, the surface of which was discernibly dryer and warmer than the gravel outside the rectangle.

She wondered aloud what had caused it.

"I don't know," he replied. "Come on."

A bearded man appeared out of the fog. He identified himself as Gregor, who lived in the nearby mill. He said he'd heard the crash ten minutes ago and had called an ambulance. Darian told him to go home and call the police and stay there until needed.

Julia covered the two miles to J.G.'s home as fast as the poor visibility allowed. They rang the bell and waited. J.G., in silk robe and pajamas, finally threw open the door. He looked wordlessly from one to the other.

"Mr Lechwood," Darian reluctantly began.

"It's my father," J.G. said hoarsely.

"No, it's your son."

"My son? My son?" he repeated dazedly.

"May we come in?" J.G. stepped back to let them pass and followed them into the living room. "Please sit down, Mr Lechwood, thank you. We found your Mercedes two miles west of here. Your son apparently drove it off the road and into a tree. I'm afraid he's dead. I'm very sorry."

J.G. silently buried his face in his hands. Darian found the phone and called the police station. Julia, suddenly afraid that she would collapse on the rug, went quickly to the front door and gulped some fresh air.

"What is it?" Jane's anxious voice came from the landing above. Julia turned to see her hovering in her wheelchair at the top of the stairs. Her husband went up and pushed her into the bedroom.

Julia could hear J.G.'s deeper voice breaking the news, and then Jane wailing, "I should have told them about the syringe! My weakness has killed him!"

"Shut up," J.G. ordered. Jane's sobbing was muffled by the closing of the door. Their words were no longer distinguishable.

"Come on, I'll take you back," Darian said.

"I couldn't possibly sleep now," Julia said.

They silently returned to the inn. He escorted her as far as her room, nodded woodenly, and was gone. The clock said half past three. She shivered into her pajamas and slid into an icy bed. When she closed her eyes she saw a smashed face biting into a bloody steering wheel. The horn blared incessantly in her ears.

She lay awake until dawn, reviewing the case. She compiled a long list of places to hide the body of a frail old man—rolled up in a rug, in a steamer trunk, cemented into a porch, dumped into a river or well; the possibilities were endless. And what about those holes in the gravel? Did Owen's accident have anything to do with his grandfather? And what about Darian? She would have to stay out of his way—but she was determined to remain in Tadbleak until the case was solved.

CHAPTER 11

AT DAWN SHE DRESSED in jeans, tee shirt and a thick sweater, and went out into the street. The fog was lifting in places. A few pigeons were pecking among the rubbish in the gutters. She'd walked only a few blocks when she recognised Harry's figure, jogging towards her. He was clad in grey sweatpants and jacket. His carrot-colored curls blew back from his face. They met in front of a bus-stop bench. He stopped, red-faced and breathing rapidly. It was several moments before he could speak.

"You're done in," he observed.

She admitted that a sleepless night had left her feeling wretched.

"Come for a jog with me. It'll refresh you. Those plimsolls will do nicely, but you'll warm up too much in that sweater—got anything respectable under it? A tee shirt? Oh, lovely." He gave her the high sign and they started out at an easy trot, conversing in snatches between breaths.

"Have you run all the way from Callingwoods?"

"Walked some, ran some. I had to get out of there. The whole household has been bonkers. First they heard Scott was at the police station for kidnapping your aunt at his secret residence. Then the news about Owen came. It was very late before everyone finally got back to bed. I hear you saw it— no wonder you couldn't sleep!"

"It was horrible. I had never seen anything—so much blood!"

"Poor rotter! Even the likes of him didn't deserve it." As they crossed the deserted green, he momentarily lost his footing on the wet grass, but gracefully caught himself.

"What was there between him and Candy?"

"She's into cocaine, and put Owen in touch with her personal chemist. J.G. suspected, I think, from something I overheard him say. He walked in on Owen and her in the garage. They were stoned and starkers, smearing car wax—"

"No—honestly! Car wax—"

"Does that shock you, my ingenuous one?"

"No actually it sounds rather nice—I like the smell. But Scott smelled of car wax. I thought it was from waxing his new Daimler . . . but—Scott and Candy? No, that's not likely . . . Go on."

"J.G. was not half berserk about that little episode. He threatened Candy. She threatened him. But J.G. doesn't let anybody lead him around by the short and curlies."

"Jane went on about her syringe before J.G. shut her up. If Owen was shooting drugs with his own mother's syringe . . ."

They were moving along a modest residential street. A dog barked from behind a fence. Across the street a pair of legs was all that could be seen—the rest of the body was in the boot of a blue Dolomite parked in front of an open garage door.

"That's Teddy Wineapple's wheels—and his legs," Harry observed. Wineapple's torso and then his face appeared, as he heard them approaching.

"Hullo." They stopped running. Julia tried a little polite chitchat but Wineapple wasn't having any. He stood very stiffly, a blank look on his delicate face, dark circles under his huge blue eyes.

"What's all this in aid of?" Harry asked, surveying the cartons of wires and tubes that cluttered the open boot.

"My hobby," Wineapple replied. He definitely looked tired —another person out and about early who hadn't gotten much sleep. "If you came to tell me about Owen—I've been informed already. J.G.'s secretary called me a half hour ago and told me no one was to come to work today." He closed the boot, unceremoniously turned his back on them and went into the garage.

"He doesn't like us very much," Julia observed, as they resumed their jog.

"He doesn't like me, you mean. And it's mutual."

Julia said that she'd sensed the resentment between them. "I thought it might be some sort of male competition thing."

"You could call it that. We played football last year on opposing teams. He kneed me in the groin—said it was an accident. I've been looking forward to returning the compliment sometime, but haven't had the pleasure."

"Without his lab coat he looks quite different. He's really rather attractive."

"If you like pasty skin and pony tails."

They ran for awhile in companionable silence. Harry praised her for keeping up the pace. "I could tell you were in good shape. Don't breathe through your mouth—it'll make your throat hurt," he instructed. She nodded. "When this bloody mess is over, I'm going back to London."

"So am I," she said.

"Good. You and I can be pals. We'll get acquainted over fish and chips—instead of stiffs and quips."

She readily agreed. He was easy company.

"Tell me about yourself, since we're going to be pals."

"Like what?" she asked.

"Family—not as tacky as mine, I assume."

"No, very normal. Mummy and Daddy were shopkeepers in Kent for twenty-five years. They're retired now. I have one sister—a geologist. She's overseas just now. We're very close."

"Any current affairs?"

"Nobody lately."

"You fancy the brainy type, don't you?"

"I suppose—but only if they have a sense of humour."

"Or an arty somebody?"

"As long as he isn't silly about it."

"Do you think poetry is silly?"

"Definitely. But I like some of it anyway—like the wry seventeenth-century stuff."

" 'But not for a lip, nor a languishing eye; she's fickle and false, and there we agree; but I am as fickle as she—' "

" 'We neither believe what either can say; and, neither believing, we neither betray,' " she concluded.

"Ah yes—jogging and Dryden, nothing can beat it for getting the old juices flowing!" he exclaimed, making a few swipes at an imaginary punching bag.

"That Cavalier stuff has always struck me as very modern —morally, that is."

He asked her if she liked Yeats. She said that she did. He quoted the opening stanza of "Song of Wandering Aengus."

"Lovely. Perfect." She sighed, "It's always been one of my favourites."

They stopped moving. Her blood was pounding, her stomach uneasy. They sat together on the steps of what was obviously the library. He unzipped his jacket. She removed her sweater.

"I get the feeling we're very much alike, you and I."

She laughed. "That's a foolproof line—no one could resist liking someone who said that."

He agreed, making a mental note to use it often. "Mother went on an astrology fad last year—that was before she was converted to the Holy Sacrament of Freud, but that's another story. She used to fix her victims with a penetrating stare like this—" He made his eyes wide and staring, like a zombie, and said huskily, "You're a Cancer, aren't you?"

"Well yes. Good guess."

"I'd recognize a fellow crab, anywhere."

"You're pulling my leg."

"No, honestly. I just had my sign legally changed to Cancer. Of course, there was an enormous amount of red tape—and a shocking fee—"

"Oh stop!" She covered his mouth with her hand. He nibbled her finger.

"Tell me about your work."

"I write advertising copy—hey, is this a video sex service interview?"

"If you like." Lifting one red eyebrow, he flashed a lubricious grin. She knew he was in earnest—as earnest as he ever was. At any rate, he was definitely easy to look at and immensely entertaining. No doubt the man knew his way around the erogenous zones like the back of his hand—but still, it wouldn't do. She fancied herself the leading lady—not just another extra in a cast of thousands.

"No," she smiled amicably, "but thank you very much indeed."

Bestowing a brotherly punch on her arm he assured her that it was okay with him. "You've got a hard case on that priggy inspector, don't you luv?"

"What—"

"Now, don't protest too much. Your pal Harry has eyes in his head. Come on, now, you can tell Harry about it."

"There's nothing to tell. Let's start back." She stood up.

"Have it your way," he shrugged. They returned to the Boar at a faster pace, too fast for further conversation. The last half mile her legs felt like lead, her lungs about to burst, but she kept the pace until they'd crossed the green. They parted in front of the inn. He patted her on the back and advised her to take a cold shower, "and you'll feel like taking on the world."

"You're all right, Harry."

He gave her the high sign again, this time in Italian, and jogged slowly off in the direction of Callingwoods. She leaned wearily against a tree and looked after him in admiration.

"My dear, you look positively drained," Lettie clucked. They were in Lettie's room, the radio on, to cover their conversation.

"I didn't sleep a wink."

"I shouldn't wonder. What were you doing out with the inspector at that late hour?" She asked, regarding her niece keenly. "I don't live in cotton wool, you know."

"He was only telling me about Scott. Will you file charges?"

"No. Stay still, Tim," she ordered, carefully running the

flea comb through his fur. "He is really a decent boy—very kind to Tim. He even went to the bother of stopping at Tesco and buying Tim's favourite brand of tinned horsemeat."

"What a magnanimous gesture."

"Hullo, there you are," Lettie gloated, cracking the flea between her nails.

"I wish you wouldn't do that in front of me."

"Do what, dear?"

Julia was on her way through the lobby as Baxter came out of the dining room from breakfast.

"I want to talk to you." He eagerly drew her into the most isolated love seat. His parka squeaked as he sat down, a noise that set her teeth on edge. "I've got something that will shake somebody's tree! Lechwood Electronics is under a video surveillance system! I found the cameras the other night when we broke in."

"Did they get us on tape?"

"No, I had a handy-dandy pocket device that interfered with their cameras while we were there." But the most interesting news was that he had located the reception center where a technician monitored the tapes.

"On Wigan Lane?" she guessed. When he looked startled and inquired how she knew, she admitted that she had seen him there.

He said that he had been staking it out for two days to determine the technician's schedule, so he would know when it was safe to break in. "It's obviously a private commercial job. This morning I hit pay dirt. I saw J.G. drop by and pay his bill. I eavesdropped. He's the money behind the surveillance for sure."

"What—if anything—does this have to do with Sir Alfred's vanishing and Owen's smashup?"

"I wish I knew! What say we put our heads together and wrap this case up?"

"I'd love to. In fact, I've got a little puzzle you might shed some light on."

"Lay it on me."

She told him about the imprints on the verge.

He listened intently, then responded, "A heavy piece of equipment with four short round legs would leave that sort of impression. The warmth and dryness of the gravel was caused by a heat source—an electric motor, ultrasound, intense light. An analysis of the gravel may—or may not—be informative."

There was a man in the phone box across the lobby whose back looked like Darian's. She relaxed when she saw his face: it was someone else. She returned her attention to the discussion. "Is it possible to build a device that would leave that sort of imprint, that would cause steering failure—or some other sort of mechanical failure—as the Mercedes passed it?"

The American looked amused and shook his head. "That's James Bond stuff—not technically feasible at this time. All the tires were intact?"

"Yes." The landlady appeared and began dusting the furniture near them. They got up and moved away. "Who are you really?" Julia whispered in his ear.

"Woodbridge Lester Baxter. Social Security Number 199-38-4174."

"What really brought you to Tadbleak?"

"Sir Alfred invited me. I'm a surveillance expert. He wasn't aware that J.G. had one operating already. Sir Alfred wanted me to design and install a system. I gather he was concerned about espionage."

"He brought you all the way from California? Why didn't he get someone here?"

"I'm the best," he said matter-of-factly.

"Congratulations."

"If you can't dazzle them with your brilliance, baffle them with your bullshit, I always say. But seriously, I really do know a helluva lot about electronics. Sir Alfred was interested in an article I wrote for a trade journal. He wrote me a letter. I wrote him back. Then he invited me across." He took an envelope from the pocket of his absurdly bulbous goosedown parka and handed it to her.

The envelope had Sir Alfred's return address at Callingwoods. "Did you reply to his office?"

"No, his home."

"Could I show this to someone who knows Sir Alfred's hand?"

"Feel free." He added that if everything went according to schedule, he would break into the video reception center at a quarter past four that afternoon to take a look at the tapes. "There's no one there until five p.m."

"I'm so glad we had this little chat. It gives me hope and I now feel that I can trust you. Don't hesitate to knock me up."

His face registered acute confusion. "I'd love to take you up on it, but—"

"Whoops, I detect another communication breakdown."

"Translate 'knock me up.' "

"Knock on my door—rouse me out."

"Take my advice, never ask an American to beat you up or knock you up, unless you're in a reckless mood."

At that moment Lettie came into the lobby waving a telegram. "It's the answer to my inquiries on Rollo's first wife's death!" she breathed, slightly red in the face. "Glad I caught you, ran all the way from the post office—quite a fag for my age . . ."

"Well?" Julia asked.

"My friend the Colonel couldn't dig up anything at all."

"You ran two blocks just to tell me that?"

"Well, I did have another motive—I wanted to interview Mr Baxter, here. He's obviously a wonderfully bright boy."

Julia left Baxter in her aunt's delicate clutches.

One of the shops that lined the street facing the green was Noreen's Curly Q. As she passed the window, Julia glanced inside and suddenly decided to have a manicure.

The interior was resplendent with gold cupids brandishing

bowls of cascading plastic geraniums. Filmy French blinds and peppermint-striped wallpaper completed the saccharine effect. Julia looked around, pretended to suddenly recognise the Oriental face under the dryer, and sociably took the chair next to hers.

Yoko ducked out from under the dryer. Her head was covered with tight pink curlers. "Hello!" she chirped in her childishly high-pitched voice. "It's going to be the new me—a frizz. How do you think I'll look?"

"Charming, I'm sure."

"I do this today. No work today, you know? The plant is closed. J.G. is at home with his wife. They're taking Owen's accident pretty hard. It has been one terrible week—first his father, then his son. It would destroy a weaker man. I worry about the Mrs—she isn't strong."

"It must have been a dreadful shock."

"Oh yes! And it's so queer about Sir Alfred! Who do you think shot at him? First they say O'Reilly—then they let him go. Why?"

Julia said she hadn't a clue.

"And what about that wire? And where did they put his body?"

Julia shrugged.

A beautician in a pink smock came over and unrolled one of her curls. "Another five minutes under the air, dearie," she said.

The secretary obediently pulled the dryer down over her head. There were a dozen women, mostly older, in various stages of shampoo and curl. Two very young pink-smocked women, with identical frost curls flipping elaborately away from their faces, were slouching over the counter, discussing social phenomena.

"I say if a man can't dance, he can't screw," the one remarked between cracks on her gum. Looking scandalized, an elderly customer nearby leaned closer to catch every word.

Julia interrupted the discussion to inquire about a manicure. They stared in blank appraisement. The one pointed to an older smocked lady who was engrossed in a gothic. "Francine does nails."

"Sorry to interrupt," Julia said to Francine, who reluctantly looked up from her book.

"Never mind. I was just getting to the part when he's about to rape her, only his horse shies."

By the time Julia had her nails done, Yoko was standing at the cash register with a full head of curls. As they left the shop together, Julia asked her if she had noticed anything odd at the plant that might shed some light on the whole nasty business.

"No," the secretary replied, raising her hand to her mouth. Something about the gesture bothered Julia. "I type all day long. No time to notice much. My boss always find too much work to get done by four o'clock." She unconsciously patted her curls. "I just notice that J.G. very tense. It's his father, after all! He try so hard to make his father slow down and act his age and not take so many risks all the time. I've seen that old man going—it must be—seventy miles an hour with nothing to protect him but a helmet and leather jacket. It is tempting fate, I say."

Wineapple had the unmistakable look of a man who had dressed in a hurry. His pale hair was not in the usual neat pony tail, but hung in a tangle to his shoulders. His beard was flat on one side. It had taken him much too long to answer the bell.

He glared and wearily expressed a fervent desire that the mystery would be cleared up so he would no longer have to tolerate these idiotic intrusions, but he had no information to impart.

She asked to use the facilities. He hesitated, then reluctantly directed her to his W.C. She was gratified that it was adjacent to the bedroom. A still-smoking cigarette, lipstick on the filter, was in the ashtray beside the bed. The bedclothes were in confusion. A bit of colour could be seen amid the sheets. It was a corner of a scarf decorated with hand-blocked batik cabbages.

Satisfying herself that there was, indeed, a back way out of the apartment, she apologized to Wineapple for the untimely intrusion and ran to the phone box on the corner. She dialled Callingwoods and asked for Lettie.

"Auntie, is Mrs. Poindexter there?"

"No, dear."

"Keep a look out and note the time she arrives home. I'll be there in fifteen minutes. We have a lot to discuss."

Lettie was sitting in front of the library fire knitting away on her growing pink bedjacket.

"Miranda arrived home ten minutes ago."

"I have good reason to believe that she and Wineapple have been getting a little on the side."

"And the gardener too? Oh my! And Wineapple is young enough to be . . ."

"I don't believe there was ever anything between her and O'Reilly. She was just using him as a ruse, or else she and Wineapple were framing O'Reilly—spreading phony rumours of an affair, then stealing one of his guns."

"But what about Jane Lechwood's description of Miranda and the gardener in the potting . . ."

"A red herring. I would suspect that Miranda told Jane that story herself—as if in spite—you know, to shock her—but with an ulterior motive to fabricate some evidence of an affair with O'Reilly. Harry says that Wineapple is also Candy's lover. Is Teddy using both women as spies to manipulate the situation for him so that he can eliminate Sir Alfred and somehow steal credit for the device? He would have a better chance than anyone else would to carry it off. Was Candy's sudden interest in Owen after he started at the plant part of this plan of Wineapple's? Or was Teddy afraid that Owen would find out what he was up to and used Candy to keep an eye on the kid?"

"It's all so muddling," Lettie sighed, knitting her brows. "Oh fudge! I dropped a purl!"

"Or is Candy behind it all, pulling Wineapple's strings? If she and Wineapple got their hands on the device, they could make a bundle and have a laugh on the Lechwoods—J.G. in particular. Perhaps Teddy was seeing Miranda on Candy's instructions." Julia's head was whirling with all the possible explanations.

"Try not to think about it for awhile, let it bubble . . ." Lettie recommended. "Jane was overwrought this morning. I got a bit out of her before J.G. came home and put a stop to it." Jane had told Lettie that upon missing her syringe, she had confronted her son with the theft. Owen had denied it. Knowing that he had lied to her before and suspecting that he was still on drugs, she feared that he had stolen her syringe to shoot heroin. She blamed herself for the accident because she was convinced that drugs had caused it.

"When did she miss the syringe?"

"The morning of November eleventh."

"The morning after Sir Alfred's visit? That's interesting."

"Why?"

"Let me think." Julia chewed her lip and fiddled with a lock of her glossy dark hair. Lettie considered her niece's wide-set brown eyes. The Chinese would say her glitter was very strong. "I got a good close look at Owen's naked arms on November eleventh—no tracks. Of course, he could have injected some other part—a thigh, say—or, he might not have started shooting the stuff at that time," Julia said after awhile.

Lettie had also heard that Jane admitted to the police that she had lied to give Owen an alibi on November 10. He'd actually left the house at two-thirty and hadn't returned until five-thirty. When she told him there was trouble she begged her to give him an alibi. She agreed on the condition that he tell her where he really had been that afternoon. He claimed he'd been deep in the Callingwoods park by the stream, smoking marijuana with Candy.

"If he really was there, he might have seen something. I

don't imagine Owen was above blackmail . . . Hmm, Candy might have seen something too—if she was really there—which might put her in danger as well—unless she's in on it."

"You aren't convinced that Owen's death was . . . ?"

"No."

Owen had received a call from a party unknown at approximately nine-thirty on the night he died. His parents heard the phone ring, heard Owen answer it, but hadn't caught anything that was said. When his parents went to bed at eleven, Owen was in his room listening to the stereo. The master bedroom was on the opposite side of the house from the garage, so they didn't hear him take the car. They claimed to have been completely unaware that he had gone out.

"When was the last they saw him that evening?" Julia asked.

"At eleven when Jane looked in his room to say good night."

There was a sound of movement in the hall. Julia opened the door in time to see Miranda on the first step. The woman paused and regarded her with unveiled hostility. Had she been eavesdropping at the door? She knows that I know about her and Wineapple, Julia thought, weighing the pros and cons of telling Miranda about Wineapple and Candy. It might work as a catalyst to clarify the lab assistant's role in the intrigue. Then again, it might clarify nothing at all and cause more unhappiness. Julia let the opportunity pass—she didn't have the intestinal fortitude for such a nasty bit of work.

CHAPTER 12

HARRY WAS IN HIS ROOM glumly juggling tennis balls in front of his mirror. He tossed them to her one at a time. She caught them and threw them back, but their act soon went awry. "A good juggler has years of practice behind him. I only took it up last week," he apologised, assuming a lotus position on the floor and bouncing a ball off his bicep. She asked him to verify that the letter Baxter had given her was indeed in his grandfather's hand.

"That's old Alf's chicken scratch, right enough. But it could be the work of a clever forger, as they say in the books—"

"Got a sample of his writing around?"

"No, but I know where I can lay my hands on one. Back in a flash." He went out. She sat on the floor and looked around at the clutter. There were a couple of very dusty model airplanes hanging by wires from the ceiling. On the wall there were posters for summer theatre—Ionesco, Brecht, that sort of thing. Harry's name was among the list of players. The furniture was littered with clothes. A few pairs of athletic socks reeked from the bookshelf above the bed. She had just noticed a mouldy apple core in a corner when he returned. They compared his sample of Alfred's writing with the letter to Baxter.

"They look the same to me. Well, thanks—" She looked at her watch.

"You aren't leaving so soon, are you?"

"I have a lot on my plate, just now," she said.

"Just stay a little while and help me with my exercises."

"What sort of exercises?"

"Don't look so suspicious. Perfectly pristine acting exercises. Give me an adjective."

"Uh—porcine."

He wrinkled up his nose and bulged his cheeks and snorted.

"Leonine."

He swelled his chest, straightened his shoulders, steeled his gaze, while tilting his head slightly.

"Not bad. Hirsute."

He arched one brow and affected a Panlike leer, while panting hoarsely. She began to giggle. There was a knock. Harry jumped up and opened the door.

Darian walked in, saw Julia, and looked extremely put out. She favoured him with her brightest, brittlest smile.

"I would like a word with you alone," he directed to Harry. "If Miss Carlisle will excuse us—" He avoided meeting her eyes.

"Of course." She stood up to leave.

"See you sometime, luv, thanks ever for the lessons," Harry called chummily.

"The pleasure was mine. Shall we work on vulpine and serpentine next time?"

"Super," he sang out and made a show of watching her walk down the hall as he recited, " 'Whenas in silks my Julia goes, then, then methinks how sweetly flows, that liquefaction of her clothes. Next, when I cast my eyes and see that brave vibration each way free, Oh, how that glittering taketh me . . .' Oh, cheer up," he told the smoldering Darian, "you can't have gravy on it every day."

"Ah, Miss Carlisle, there you are," the butler greeted her in the hall. "A phone call for you." He showed her into the morning room. She sat at the desk and lifted the receiver. There was a click as the butler hung up the hall phone.

"Baxter here. Mission accomplished." He sounded wildly elated. "I got a look at some dynamite tapes! There's a hidden camera inside Wineapple's lab. The tape was dated November tenth p.m. Sir Alfred's door opens—it's the old man himself coming out of his lab. He stumbles slightly and bumps against a lab table. Then he reaches in his pocket and pulls out a little beauty that could be his latest brainchild. He looks it over very carefully, as if to reassure himself that he didn't damage it when he bumped it. Then he returns it to his pocket and walks out of view of the camera."

"How can you be certain it was Sir Alfred, when you've never met him?"

"I've seen photos—but don't you get it—"

"Yes. Sir Alfred may have had his invention on his person on the fateful day."

"Right. There were two other interesting tapes. One dated November twelfth was of Wineapple carrying out a piece of apparatus—about the size of the rectangle you found on the gravel near Owen's crash."

"What was it?"

"I couldn't tell. It was in a carton—but I can guess. Hold onto your seat—the tape machine operates all day and night. Last night it picked up an outrageous kind of interference— video equipment can be very sensitive to certain bands. It looked like a pair of headlights approaching out of the dark at a rapid rate—like a car racing towards the point of view."

"So?"

"Do I have to draw you a diagram? If you were driving in the fog at night and saw what looked like a car in your lane racing towards you, what would you do?"

"Brake and swerve."

"And if it kept coming at you, you'd have no choice but to go off the road and into the trees."

"I see—but I don't see. How?"

"To create such an illusion, you'd need a laser projector, a portable power pack, a video camera—plus the fog to project it on. It would be a simple matter, for anyone who knew what he was doing, to form a live feedback loop and project it onto the fog—it wouldn't work without the water particles reflecting a simple image like that. It would create an electronic mirror—with Owen's own headlights appearing to be those of another approaching car, one that keeps coming right for him, no matter how he maneuvers to avoid it. The power pack would have four little legs and would be about the same size of the imprint. It would create a fair amount of heat."

Julia found herself excitedly skipping around the desk. "Who would have access to the equipment and know how to use it?"

"It's all there at Lechwood's plant. Like I said, Wineapple might have been carrying it out right in front of the camera."

"But you didn't get a close enough look at it to be certain?"

"No. His back was to the camera; it blocked my view of the apparatus. Back to your question who would know how to use it—someone with a related technical background."

"J.G., Wineapple, and you."

"And rock technicians."

"What does geology have to do with this?"

"Nothing. I mean the guys who produce light shows at rock concerts—roadies. They've recently started using laser projectors to create spectacular visuals."

"Owen told me Candy introduced him to one of The Sickies—so she might have the connections—and the knowhow."

"One other thing, someone has made a splice on November twelfth—they've cut something out of the tape."

"Hmm! That puts a different perspective on what remains on the film, doesn't it? It suggests that something thoroughly incriminating was removed. There's a wealth of implications there . . . give me time to mull this one over. Can we risk breaking into the tapes again? I'd like to see for myself."

"If he's true to schedule, the technician will go for an hour dinner break at seven. I'll be parked somewhere on Wigan Lane. Meet you at my car at seven fifteen."

Julia returned to the library. Lettie was still in front of the fire, but had set her knitting aside and rested her head against the back of the chair.

"Are you tired, Auntie?"

"Just a little, dear. Maybe I'm too old for so much . . ."

Julia described, as best she could, Baxter's tape discoveries and his theory of how Owen's smash might have been engineered.

"You mean they did it with mirrors?" Lettie held her head, obviously taken aback with such technology.

"Something like that—but like a video mirror—with a camera."

"A movie camera?"

"No, a television camera, I think," Julia replied. "It would explain the marks on the verge and the headlight tape Baxter saw."

"But think of the risk of being seen while setting the camera up!"

"It was late at night and foggy."

"Still—I don't like it." Lettie frowned.

"So the murderer had some nerve as well as technical knowledge and imagination."

"A simple little revolver can be tossed in the river—but this camera business . . ."

"Remember the dark and the fog," Julia reiterated patiently. "It is interesting that there was no sign of anyone or their equipment when we looked over the scene. Could have been hiding—"

"And how soon after the smash was that?"

"About ten minutes, if that man Gregor is accurate."

"Tell me how far the marks were from the bridge."

"About fifteen or twenty ~~years~~ YARDS. The fog was especially thick there! According to Baxter, fog is the screen required for the image to be successfully visible."

"There's always more fog around a river—I wonder . . ."

Julia waited, but Lettie would not elaborate. Shrugging, Julia said that she had to be off. Lettie scooped up her knitting and murmured something about stirring up a little trouble. The two parted on the front porch with a mutual warning to be careful. *How'd they get there?*

Lettie carefully kept her eyes from the man's bathrobe that threatened to fall open at any moment. She had never approved of women who wore men's clothes—or vice versa, for that matter. Candy, unconcerned with her unladylike attire, held a mirror in front of her face and plucked her brows. It was quite a job, as she plucked every single hair and penciled two exaggerated thin arches in a peculiar colour of sable that didn't go with her platinum frizz.

"You and I must have a little talk . . ." Lettie reluctantly began, feeling ill at ease with this brash creature.

"So talk," the girl said to her mirror, "Ow, that one made my eye water!"

Obviously the poor thing had no upbringing, Lettie thought, and said, "I have it on good authority that you were with Owen in the park on the afternoon of November tenth . . ."

"I already told the cops that I was here all the time with my hubby."

"It wasn't wise to lie."

Candy stopped plucking, lowered the mirror slightly, and glared. "Some cheek you've got, coming into my house and calling me a liar."

"I only came here because I fear for your welfare."

"My eye! You came here because you're a nosey old Parker!" she said tartly.

Lettie pressed her lips together in a thin line and counted to ten. Candy resumed depilating. Lettie studied the girl's ear —very rounded at the top and cupped forward slightly—a sure sign of gross sensuality, if she'd ever seen one. "Believe what you like, my dear," she carefully replied, "but hear this —there is evidence that Owen was murdered last night— possibly because of something he saw on November tenth. If you saw it too, your life isn't worth a . . ."

Candy dropped her mirror and stared. "It was a car accident."

"It was made to look that way."

"How?"

"I am not at liberty to say. Has it occurred to you that J.G.

is inclined to believe his son's death was due to drug abuse? He claims to have evidence that Owen got his drugs through you. He might have you arrested."

Candy's eyes narrowed to slits as she shrieked, "Did that frigging bastard send you over here to threaten me?! That tears it, I'll fix his ass for him!"

Lettie gasped at her language and longed to bolt for the door, but held firm. "J.G. is a very powerful man."

"And what am I? I'm no natural lickspittle, I can tell you! I've got the goods on him, I have!" This idea obviously gratified her immensely. She took one last look at what were once her brows in the mirror, then took up nail-polish remover and cotton balls and carefully sponged the color from her toenails. Lettie noticed she had a very prominent big toe. What ancient Chinese texts would make of this, she wasn't certain. "Wait now, if Owen really was murdered, his father would be the first suspect I'd check into!" the girl declared maliciously.

"You sound as if you have some damaging information on J.G. that the police might . . ."

"Not by half I do! The time might be ripe to play my hand. That bastard better pull his socks up if he wants to win this one!" She chuckled, displaying what would have been a malevolent sneer if the effect hadn't been spoiled by jutting incisors.

In the wan light the river foamed deep and swift beneath the bridge. The old mill looked deserted and about to cave in under a mass of vines. Lettie made her way through the nettle-choked garden and rapped on the door. Gregor, the artist who inhabited the place, eventually poked his head out an upstairs window. "Go away!" he shouted.

"Just a few minutes of your time. It's about last night's dreadful car smash."

"I don't know anything." He pulled his head in and slammed the window closed.

"Oh charming!" Lettie grumbled and banged louder on

the door, but he wouldn't answer. Finding the door unlocked, she paused a moment to muster enough cheek to barge in. Her heart pounded. It was the rudest act of her life, but there was nothing for it. She was nervously surveying the chaos of the dark, littered living room when Gregor came bolting down the stairs.

"Trespassers!" he snarled. "They park behind my wall, they take snaps of each other in my garden, but never have they had the gall to walk right into my house before!"

She surveyed his wild hair and beard and told him he looked exactly how she'd always imagined John the Baptist must have looked. This information didn't seem to mollify him very much, so she got right down to brass tacks. "You must tell me what you know about last night. It's urgent."

"Get out."

"It's a matter of life and death, otherwise I never would have . . ."

Gregor rolled his eyes heavenward and cursed, a gesture that made him look even more biblical, somehow.

She sat down in a moth-eaten old rocker. "I won't leave until you answer two questions. First of all, what did you hear or see last night? And have you noticed anyone loitering about the last few days—or anything at all out of the ordinary?"

The artist fussed and fumed, but finally was no match for Lettie's relentless perspicacity. "I was working late in my upstairs studio when I heard a horn and the sound of a collision at about half past two. I called the ambulance and went out to see if anything was to be done before they arrived. I ran into Inspector Darian, who had just arrived at the scene, was instructed to go home and did so. An ambulance came by, then more police cars. Darian came back and interviewed me then. I explained that I had heard only one car, the horn, then a terrible crash. I also told him that I haven't noticed anyone around here lately but a couple of fishermen from Tadbleak, whom I know personally. Now get out, or I will bodily tip you out on your ancient bum!"

Taking deep breaths to calm herself, Lettie prowled the scene of the smash. The wreck had been taken away, but a splintered tree trunk and broken glass marked the spot. The telltale marks on the verge were covered over by a confusion of footprints. The police had obviously been all over the area, but she walked around anyway, hopeful of finding something they'd overlooked. She shuffled along the verge, worrying at the murderer's problem.

The road dropped rapidly in a series of curves. Because of the terrain, there were no lay-bys, or even enough verge to safely park a car anywhere in the valley around the river. And that, Lettie thought, was precisely the murderer's problem. If he hadn't parked near the mill where Gregor would have heard him drive past, where had he left his vehicle? Julia had said that the three pieces of equipment involved would weigh eighty pounds or so, altogether. Too heavy a burden to carry on one's back for more than a few yards! A cycle of any sort would have been perilously overloaded.

She walked across the bridge, then back again, determined to work this point out. The murderer might have made a previous foray in a car and secreted the equipment somewhere. It would have to be nearby because of the weight, but well enough concealed so that a passing angler did not stumble across the hiding place. The area was well tramped by local fishermen.

This particular river would never find its way into *Great Trout Streams of the British Isles.* There were no trout or salmon. Lettie wasn't certain what the dour types loitering about the banks were dangling their hooks after. But anyone familiar with the lay of the land would realise the danger of discovery, should he try to bury or disguise the equipment in the vicinity. In fact, it seemed odd that any local would have chosen this spot for a murder, despite the necessary atmospherics. It was a curious business—much more than just a little wire strung across a driveway and a missing body. That, of course, was a simple matter of legerdemain; but this video camera business was sadistically technical. She didn't like it at all.

From under the bridge came a wet, clumping sound, punctuated by a pleasant whir. Lettie slipped into the gap between the bank and the abutment, carefully edging down the shallow riverbank where a big, husky lad was casting his line into a pool. His heavy boots squelched as he shifted his weight.

"Hello young man."

He looked up and scowled in the time-honoured manner of all interrupted fishermen. "Mum."

"What are you fishing for?" She peered into his damp haversack, where something silvery was gasping out its life. "Is that a whitefish? I've never learned to identify any of them without the sauces . . ." she chirped, hoping to break enough ice to pump him for anything out of the way he might have noticed.

"Whitefish is shark."

"Shark!" She could not help but snort. "My, my! These waters run deep!"

"Shark," he repeated indignantly. "From dur ocean."

"The sea?" She thought for a moment. "You mean *this* is not a whitefish, which actually comes from the sea?"

"And it be shark."

"Not this, I presume." Lettie furrowed her brow. "I believe I see. A whitefish is actually a shark, then?"

"Ar."

"Delightful." To think that she had been eating whitefish for decades, never guessing it was really some primal beast that had probably fed upon human flesh off Zanzibar, or worse, off Australia! Indeed! Thoroughly disgusted, she resumed the heavy going at hand. "So, what . . . sort of thing have you been catching then?"

"Pump" it sounded like.

"Pump?"

"Ar." He hooked a thumb over his shoulder at something wet and muddy leaning against a tree. It was, indeed, a good-sized tire pump, the sort used for emergency repairs on the road. Not a surprising thing to find in a river. Then a thought, elusive as a minnow, swam into her stream of consciousness.

With a triumphant cry, she caught it. The fisherman gave her a sharp look.

"Very nice!" She grabbed the pump and clutched it dripping to her bosom, as her brain feverishly clicked away.

Lettie hurried back to Callingwoods. She had a sudden, compelling urge to build some toy boats. A real boat would be needed, too, as well as an oarsman. No doubt O'Reilly would be just the man for the job.

Baxter's car was empty. There was no one on the street. Mentally flagellating herself for not asking him exactly where the reception center was located, Julia stood where he'd been parked the previous evening. Across the street in the direction he had been surveying were a shabby boarding house, a laundry, and a garage.

She rang the door of the boarding house. An inebriated old Irish woman let her in and handed her a gin. There was a loud party in progress on the first floor. A mob of people were milling around, drinks in hand; music was blaring from the stereo. She sipped her drink and spent what seemed an eternity gossiping to satisfy herself that there were no recent tenants who might be hiding a lot of video equipment in a room there.

She slipped away from the gaiety and prowled around the dark garage next door, but couldn't find a way in. The laundry, a two-story structure, was also dark. There was a flight of stairs off a dead-end alley, which was partially lit by a nearby street light. She cautiously flashed her torch along every inch of wall and pavement. An instinctive alarm system went off in a gland—probably just the memory of a similar dark alley and a blow to the head; but there it was, impossible to ignore.

There were a dozen rubbish bins at the back. In a dark corner behind the cans, she saw a limp bag of clothes which the torch revealed to be Baxter.

He was lying in a pool of blood. A red, spreading stain darkened the front of his white sweater. She felt his pulse—

he was still alive. She tore off her jacket and bound it tightly against his chest with a rope she made from their belts. During the process, she found herself muttering all the words of encouragement that she'd ever heard. "Easy now. You can do it. Stiff upper lip. It'll be right. Not to worry. Just a flesh wound. Nothing serious. Oh my God, please don't die!"

She ran back to the boarding house and shouted above the din into the hall phone for an ambulance, then dashed back to grab a towel in the Austin's boot to use to apply more pressure to Baxter's wound. An impulse to faint came and went. A rat scuttled among the rubbish just a few inches from her face. A rotten miasma drifted around the mess.

There was the siren. Fearing that perhaps she hadn't given them specific enough directions, she ran out into the street and waved them over.

The hospital again—the same white uniforms, the same disorientation but worse this time—worse than a sickening headache. She felt a horrible constriction in the throat and stomach. "He isn't going to die, is he?"

"Sit down miss. You look a bit peaked."

"Is he going to die?" The nurse only compressed her lips, her eyes acquiring a professional evasiveness.

They pushed him down the hall on a gurney, leaving her to shiver and bite her nails in the lobby. The white neon flickered and buzzed, creating the effect of a migraine—appropriate atmosphere for an anxiety attack.

Review the facts. Arrange and rearrange. Make sense of it. There had been so much blood. She suddenly noticed the stains on her clothing. There had been so much in the alley. There had been a lot of Owen's blood in the Mercedes . . . but so little of Sir Alfred's on the drive. Who would have thought the old man would have so little blood in him?

Who killed Owen? Someone with the technical know-how and access to a laser projector. Who killed Sir Alfred? Someone who had seen the surveillance tape of the old man carrying the device out of the lab that day. Was there time to see the tape, decide to kill him for it, drive to O'Reilly's, steal a gun, secrete the car, and hide in the park? The drive from Wigan Lane to O'Reilly's couldn't take more than ten minutes. It could be done if X had seen the tape by 4:30. X fired and missed, ran, threw the gun away. But would X have also strung up the wire?

Then Owen contacted X—blackmail. X couldn't risk letting Owen live, so he acquired the necessary equipment and waited for the fog . . . Did X get the equipment at the plant? Had he returned it yet?

J.G. knew about the cameras, could have seen the tape that day; but would he shoot his father? And would Owen, in turn, blackmail his own father? Would J.G. murder his own son? From what little she had observed of them, it didn't strike her as completely unlikely.

But what explained the wire and Sir Alfred vanishing? Inconsistencies . . . the syringe. Start at the beginning . . . of course! The manuscript! Julia groaned and snapped her fingers. Her sole source of information! The dog! It was all falling into place! That airy-fairy nonsense about the poison and the gunshot being the key!

"Nurse! I must leave immediately—but please—is there any word of my friend?"

"He is in intensive care, but Doctor just informed me that he's holding his own."

"Thank you. I'll return later tonight. If he wakes up—tell him I've solved it."

CHAPTER 13

SHE COULD NEVER RECALL a moment of the drive to St Martin's. That night remained in her memory as a white agonizing blur of slow minutes, then a flash of comprehension, then a nervous period of darkness and suddenly she was entering her aunt's garden. The huge brown head of the Great Dane peered out the kitchen window at her, his black jowls trailing slobber on the glass. He bared his teeth and barked a booming warning. A light glowed dimly through the drawn living-room drapes.

When there was no response to the bell, she let herself in with her latchkey. A deep, ferocious rumble greeted her. The Dane only allowed her a few feet inside.

She grabbed the welcome mat, using it as a shield, as she said in a soothing voice, "Think tranquil thoughts . . . concentrate on your breathing . . ." She edged forward several steps. The dog bared his teeth.

"It's Julia Carlisle, please call off the dog!" she called.

A tiny, wizened face peeked at her from the other room. "You look just like the photograph on the piano. Heel, Rex, heel." Rex reluctantly heeled. "Take him into the kitchen and feed him a Pup Yummie. It'll cement your relationship."

Julia warily took a few steps. The beast's breath was warm on her back as they went through the swinging kitchen door. "Quick, where are the biscuits, before he does something we'll both regret."

"In the jar, top of the fridge."

She quickly left the dog in the kitchen, devouring biscuits. The old man had settled into the rocker in the living room.

"Sir Alfred Lechwood, I presume?"

"Clever girl! But, hell's teeth!" he gasped. "You're injured!"

"No. It's Baxter's blood, not mine."

"They didn't get Baxter too!"

"Shot, I think, but he's in hospital and hanging on."

"Touch wood. Poor boy. I never even got to meet him—will he survive?"

"I hope so. I'm very glad to find *you* alive and well! Why the hell didn't Lettie let me in on this?!"

"I made her swear to divulge my whereabouts to no one. I couldn't risk trusting anybody."

"You could have trusted me, for God's sake."

"How could I know? I knew nothing about you," he shrugged. "But how did you discover my hidey hole?"

"Well, I never bought that wire routine. It was much too stagey and really, I beg your pardon, there just wasn't enough blood about to convince . . . not to mention the shocking lack of corpse."

"So sorry."

"But, even then, I'm ashamed to say, I didn't recognise the significance of *Murder After Tea-Time* until this evening. When I read it, I didn't know how much was fact or fiction. When I arrived on the scene and the Great Dane (in the handy-dandy closed dog carrier) was nowhere to be seen, I assumed that it was just one of Lettie's fictitious touches, and thought no more about it. But tonight I recalled the Brighton cousins mentioning that the Crabtree-Swipes had been suddenly called to Canada—perhaps they had asked Lettie to look after their big dog while they were gone. That linked to Lettie's housekeeper's remark that she was glad Lettie had taken 'that awful dog with her.' I'd assumed at the time that she was at last revealing a deep-seated loathing of dear little Tim."

The old man giggled. "It was cozy in that carrier, I'll tell you! I had to feed Rex two boxes of Pup Yummies to keep him smiling. Even so, I got a nasty bruise where he stepped on my leg."

"That must have been nerve-racking! I also realised tonight that Lettie was initially my sole source of information on the events that took place preceding my arrival. I trusted her implicitly, of course. It never occurred to me that the crafty old thing might be holding out on me."

"It made her most uncomfortable, I'm sure."

"But why the wild plot?"

"I was convinced that one of my relatives had attempted to poison me."

"It never occurred to you that Sparky could be the intended —as well as the actual—victim."

"I'm not so clever as you, little one." He turned his palms up apologetically. "I was terrified. I couldn't endure the prospect of remaining in my own house, waiting for the axe to fall. And the thought of living for the rest of my life under police protection was intolerable! After the poisoning Lettie came to my door in the early hours of the morning when I was beyond despair, and offered her help. I let her in. She had always been trustworthy when I had known her as a girl, and I liked her looks. Besides, she didn't have anything to gain from my early demise."

is that not early?

"Early demise—you're seventy-two, aren't you?"

He nodded. "A mere seventy-two. Lettie and I plotted a slight legerdemain that night—a bizarre trap, she called it."

"Lettie's idea—I thought so."

"I would mysteriously disappear under sinister circumstances, which would get me safely away and attract a thorough police investigation. I intended that the viper in my house would be caught before it struck again!"

"You visited Jane in order to steal her syringe."

"Yes, I needed it to draw out a little of my blood—too little, you say. But, at my age, you need every drop just to wake up in the morning. Under the pretense of using the W.C., I nicked the syringe out of the medicine chest."

"I suspected as much."

"Meanwhile Lettie was setting the stage. She told my sister that the Crabtree-Swipes had returned and requested their dog shipped back by rail. She took the wire from the potting shed and hid it under the tenth tree from the end of the drive.

In the early afternoon she put Rex into his dog carrier and drove off on a leisurely shopping expedition. I went home at tea-time and stayed in my room until my usual time to return to the plant.

"The light was fading as I rode down the driveway. I saw no one. It gave me a bad turn when I felt something tear my trousers and looked down to see a bullet hole in the tank! I nearly fell off from the shock!"

"Were you wearing a helmet?"

"Yes—contrary to habit—but I intended to ditch the bike and wore a helmet as an extra precaution."

"That's it, then!" she exclaimed triumphantly.

"You mean you know who took a shot at me?"

"Yes—and who murdered Owen and shot Baxter—and hit me on the head, although I shouldn't complain."

The old man clenched his fists, breathing noisily. His faded blue eyes widened, causing him to resemble an intently startled bird of prey. "Don't dwaddle, girl—tell me!"

"In a moment. Just a few more loose ends to clear up. Was the gadget you had in your pocket that day the fabled recent invention?"

He answered in the affirmative and removed from the sagging pocket of his ancient green cardigan an unimpressive-looking bit of glass. It was a narrow tube less than two inches long with a spring and a few other bits of hardware inside.

"So what happened after the bullet just missed your leg?"

Although badly shaken, he said, he had managed to stick to the plan. He parked his cycle, strung up the wire, and planted the necessary evidence. Then he remounted, leaned forward to get under the wire, dumped the bike, and ran for cover. He waited in the trees at a prearranged spot along the road a few yards west of the pillars. Lettie drove up a few minutes later and picked him up. She gave him a key and a letter to her housekeeper. He stayed out of sight in the back seat, feeding Rex snacks until they'd almost reached the train station, at which time he got into the carrier with the dog. There were a few tense moments of negotiation, but fortunately Rex accepted the invasion of his privacy philosophically. Lettie had the porter dolly the carrier into the freight van, warning him not to open the lid even an inch, for fear of releasing her two vicious dogs. She made arrangements for the carrier to be delivered directly to the cottage door. The housekeeper was somewhat startled when she opened the lid and saw Sir Alfred and Rex curled up together like a pair of sardines, but soon calmed down and accepted the situation gracefully.

Julia, who had been pacing back and forth in front of the hearth during the narrative, now stopped and propped her elbow on the mantel, a satisfied smile on her face.

"Well, speak up, girl, I have—"

The shattering of the glass terrace door made them both start violently. A muzzle of a revolver pointed at them through the hole in the glass. Then a dainty hand reached through and turned the door knob.

"Don't move, please," Yoko giggled.

Sir Alfred cried out. Rex, barking furiously, burst through the kitchen door and lunged for the intruder's throat. Julia grabbed knickknacks from the mantel and hurled them at the secretary's black curls. Yoko aimed and fired, but the smashing missiles prevented her shot from hitting the dog. Screaming, she fell to the floor, the dog on top of her. Julia had the gun and Sir Alfred was yelling "Heel, Rex!" as Darian and a small army of underlings appeared, followed by Lettie bubbling something about rubber rafts.

"Julia—Julia! Are you all right?" Darian cried, his voice shaking.

CHAPTER 14

"HOW LONG HAVE YOU KNOWN Sir Alfred was at St Martin's?" Julia demanded, indignation coloring her cheeks.

"Now, don't bristle! I've known for a day or two. Oh—cheer up! I had several advantages over you—namely a dozen men, not to mention the fact that I didn't have your aunt to fool me with shrewd little tarafiddles. Routine checking of everybody's whereabouts at the time of the crime led me to your aunt—to the train station—to the porter—to St Martin's."

"You could have told me."

"But I wasn't at all certain you didn't know all along—you made some remarks that could be interpreted along those lines. I was waiting for *you* to tell *me.*"

"So you could sneer and say 'Oh, I've known that for days'?" She narrowed her eyes in disgust. "You'd have loved that, wouldn't you?"

Darian threw back his head, convulsing with mirth. She considered pointing out a patch on his neck that he had missed shaving. "Besides," he said, still grinning, "you can count coup when it comes to Yoko Okawa. What made you suspect her?"

"Half a tick—first tell me how she and you both converged on St Martin's so hard upon my heels?"

"I rushed to the hospital when I heard about Baxter's shooting. You had gone, but I persuaded the nurse to repeat your message. 'I've solved it' could have implied that you had just deduced that Sir Alfred was at Lettie's. Or you could have a hot lead on the sniper and were up to some absurdly dangerous machinations. I called Callingwoods, in case you were there. I talked to Lettie, who was gloating over a raft she'd found downstream from Owen's smash, which she insisted explained the transport of video equipment. She was so elated, I had the devil's time interesting her in my alarm over you. She finally heard what I was saying and insisted I take her along to look for you. Anyway, I had every policeman in Tadbleak searching for any sign of you, but I couldn't tolerate just waiting to hear word; so on a hunch, I drove to St Martin's. During the drive Lettie rattled on about toy boats to analyse currents and nonsensical tricks with video mirrors. I couldn't make head nor tails of it, but I was extremely anxious. In fact, the only way I managed to keep my spirits up during the bloody interminable drive was by fantasizing a rescue scene—the worst sort of mawkish treacle."

Fascinated, she asked, "What sort of the worst sort of mawkish treacle?"

He pursed his lips and looked abashed, "It's damned puerile—but effective . . ."

"Out with it."

"I arrive on my white charger, snatch you from the jaws of danger, and ride off, carrying you, properly enchanted, away in my arms. Wait—before you laugh—I was under too much strain to come up with something original."

"I wasn't going to laugh."

"You were—see—you can't keep a straight face, you devil!" Shaking his head, he looked at the ceiling in a comic gesture of exasperation.

"Well, I *am* amused—but touched as well," she quietly added.

"As I intended you to be," he said solemnly.

"I'm aware of that," she replied. He opened his mouth to protest, but she continued, "Never mind. Tell me how Yoko figured out Sir Alfred's whereabouts?"

"She didn't. She followed you. She must have been hiding somewhere near the alley. Now, *you* tell *me*—when did the penny drop?"

"As I was sitting in the hospital lobby—everything suddenly clicked. I remembered that she had let slip something about seeing Sir Alfred wearing a helmet. I had it from several sources that the old man never wore one. I deduced that either Yoko had never actually seen him on his motorcycle and just assumed that he wore a helmet, or she had actually seen him wearing one and didn't realise it was a revealing exception to his habits. It seemed logical that Sir Alfred might wear a helmet if he anticipated taking a voluntary spill—which supported my suspicions that the wire was just a gimmick—which lead me to believe that Yoko might have been on the scene after tea-time November tenth."

"There must be more."

"Of course. As J.G.'s secretary, she might have known about Sir Alfred's invention and J.G.'s secret video surveillance system—so she could have had access to the video tapes and the laser projector. Also, I had a Japanese friend in college. She told me a little about Japanese body language—"

"No! Not body language!" he protested.

"I know it's too au courant for words—but there it is. My friend said that if a Japanese giggles and puts his hand over his mouth as he speaks, these could be indications of something contradictory or embarrassing . . . So, I suspected Okawa had lied to me. Be that as it may—I assumed that she discovered from the tape that Sir Alfred had his invention on him and decided to shoot him for it."

"Mmm hmm. My foreign sources tell me she has an uncle in Tokyo who would pay her a bundle for it. She'd worked several years in his factory over there—so she knows a diode when she sees one," he said.

"She spliced out the incriminating evidence of herself borrowing a laser projector?"

"Presumably. The video equipment was found down river, near where your aunt found the rubber raft. Yoko intended to return the stuff piece by piece to the plant. The revolver she pointed at you was the same one she used on Baxter."

"So what gadget did the camera catch Wineapple lifting?"

He shrugged. "Some sort of apparatus to play with at home."

"You don't know what it is, do you?" She grinned. "I'll ask Baxter, he'll explain it to me—at length."

"Baxter turned into a puppy dog when you entered that hospital room this morning."

"I didn't notice."

"No, of course not."

"He walked in on Yoko while she was rerecording the tape —but what exactly was she up to?" Julia asked.

"According to Baxter, she'd spliced out the bit of tape showing her lifting the laser projector—but it was obvious that a splice had been made. She was recording it onto a new tape, which would eliminate all evidence of the splice. She hadn't had a chance to look at the tapes since the murder, so she knew nothing about the incriminating headlamp interference. Baxter broke in. She pulled a gun, marched him down the stairs and in the alley shot him. No one heard the shot."

"The party next door."

"And a silencer. The surgeon said he would have probably died in another hour if you hadn't saved him."

"But why didn't she just destroy the tape instead of splicing and rerecording it?"

"Each tape is coded and numbered. Each is an exact length. She couldn't risk the attendant finding out that someone had tampered with the tapes, for fear that it would implicate her."

Julia nodded. "So J.G. knew that she was aware of the surveillance system?"

"Yes. You are such a bright girl! I keep remarking on it, because it keeps amazing me. I suppose I'd eventually grow accustomed to it," he mused, questions and answers playing across his face.

"Of course you would—bored by it, even," she added evilly.

"Cynical as hell, aren't you?" He seemed undecided whether to be chagrined or amused.

"Only in self-defense. But let's not talk about us; let's talk about them. What's Candy got on J.G.?"

"She hasn't revealed it to us yet. Waiting for the optimum moment, so she can milk it for all it's worth, no doubt."

"Blast! I so wanted all the loose ends tidied up! That telegram from Lettie's retired colonel was unsatisfactory on Rollo's first wife's death. I don't suppose we'll ever know the truth of that matter either. Oh well. What about the Wineapple triangle?"

Darian visibly tensed. Since her speech on the subject, infidelity was a sore point between them, which made the Lechwood's philandering ways a touchy subject. With obvious reluctance, Darian told her that Giles had accused his wife of adultery and demanded to know the other man's identity. To protect Wineapple—it would be the end of his job if anyone found out—Miranda went about giving everyone the impression that O'Reilly was her lover, a ruse that put the gardener in a terrible spot. He had impulsively poisoned Sparky (Beatrice planned to file charges against him for that). To make matters worse, he didn't have an alibi for the time Sir Alfred was supposedly killed. And, thanks to Miranda, he appeared to have a motive. Miranda was afraid the gardener would be hanged for a crime that she had inadvertently framed him for, but she was reluctant to implicate Wineapple.

"And while Miranda was protecting her lover's employment record, he was having another affair—with Candy! Small wonder they're both after his blood, now that they've found out what he's been up to! If I were him, I'd leave town. Lettie tells me that the Poindexter marriage is definitely on the rocks. And Candy and Rollo are discussing divorce. You know, I read somewhere that the triangle is the strongest structure—but obviously not in human affairs—"

"Dammit!" he snapped. "You needn't bludgeon me with it! Tomorrow when I get back to London I'll see her straight away. I'll explain that I'm not ready for marriage. I'll break it off."

"Will you?"

Agitated, he turned his back on her searching gaze, got out of bed, and fumbled into his powder-blue underwear.